D1041228

HIS WOMAN'S GIFT

Lacey Dancer

A KISMET® Romance

METEOR PUBLISHING CORPORATION

Bensalem, Pennsylvania

KISMET® is a registered trademark of Meteor Publishing Corporation

Copyright © 1993 S.A. Cook
Cover Art Copyright © 1993 William Graf

All rights reserved.

No part of this book may be reproduced, stored in a retrieval system, or transmitted in any form, by any means, including mechanical, electronic, photocopying, recording or otherwise, without prior written permission of the publisher, Meteor Publishing Corporation, 3369 Progress Drive, Bensalem, PA 19020.

First Printing August 1993.

ISBN: 1-56597-078-0

All the characters in this book are fictitious. Any resemblance to actual persons, living or dead, is purely coincidental.

Printed in the United States of America.

LACEY DANCER

Lacey Dancer is a dream weaver. Her age is according to the day and the problems belonging to that moment. Her goals are to give to others the best of herself and to her work more than she did the day before. Her life is mated with one man's, for now a quarter of a century of loving. From that love came two children who alternately make her proud and drive her nuts. But that's living and loving by the choices she has made.

Other books by Lacey Dancer:

No.   7   *SILENT ENCHANTMENT*
No. 35   *DIAMOND ON ICE*
No. 49   *SUNLIGHT ON SHADOWS*
No. 59   *13 DAYS OF LUCK*
No. 77   *FLIGHT OF THE SWAN*
No. 98   *BABY MAKES FIVE*
No. 127   *FOREVER JOY*
No. 133   *LIGHTNING STRIKES TWICE*

PROLOGUE

The auditorium was packed to capacity, the crowd murmuring as it awaited the appearance of the guest speaker, Eve Noble. The announcer walked from stage left to center, cleared his throat and the gathering quieted expectantly.

"Ladies and gentlemen, thank you for joining us today to greet and listen to a very special young woman, Eve Noble. A woman whose courage and determination has done much to make us, the hearing public, aware of those different from ourselves only in their inability to perceive sound in the ordinary way. By her example and her firsthand experience of the nonhearing world, she has shown us that what was once a disability or handicap is only a different brand of living, that being deaf is not the sum of another human being, that there is a good and productive life waiting for anyone who wishes to meet the challenges that all of us face in one form or another. I know you all will share my very great joy

7

in having Eve with us." He turned to his right, smiling proudly as he held out his hand in welcome.

Eve glided onto the stage, smiling at the audience that she couldn't hear. She was a fragile woman, barely five feet two, slender to the point of thinness. Her eyes looked large, impossibly wide with a serene expression that conveyed the idea that their owner had never known the gut-numbing effects of true pain, the disillusionment of betrayal or the defeat of circumstances beyond human control. Her smile was gentle, loving in a way that touched everyone with whom she came in contact. Without speaking a word she filled space with her presence and her warmth. The audience felt the effect right down to its collective toes. As one, the automatic applause that had greeted her entrance drifted away. No coughs or fidgets marred the silence as Eve took the announcer's place at the podium.

"Thank you for inviting me to share this time with you." Eve's words were easily understandable, faintly inflected, and richly toned. The only hint that her hearing was not all it should be was in the delicate blurring around the edges of the syllables. The small flaw was lost in the power of her presence and her confidence. "And for caring enough, those of you who can hear, to listen and to want to learn and understand more of my world. In spite of what you might think, it is a beautiful world, in some ways more beautiful than your own. Silence isn't a prison unless one makes it so. Think for a moment. Think of all the noise that fills your mind to overflowing on any one given day. Machines, sirens, conversation, even noise in an auditorium like this," she said, looking straight at the gathering, finding individual faces, caring faces, curious faces, needing faces. As she spoke she signed her words, her slender hands moving with a grace and elegance that was more beautiful and expressive than the loveliest music.

"Because I had my hearing until the age of six I have experience in both our worlds. Yes, I lost something when my illness created complications that stole my ability to perceive sound as most others do. But I didn't lose the ability to feel, to wish, to hope, to dream. I did not become less human, less a woman. Now, I have two ways to communicate in one language. That is more than most, not less. I can concentrate without being interrupted by sound. That's more, not less. I can understand others in ways I might not ever have learned without this so-called disability. I have learned to see more of my world and yours than I ever would have known existed had it been clouded with the multitude of sounds that every day brings into our lives."

She paused then continued, letting her truth sink into the minds of those who had come to learn, to understand. There were always a number of nonhearing people in her audiences, some bitter over what had been denied them, some just apathetic, others curious about her life and how it differed from the ones they had made. Family members of the deaf came to gain support, to try to understand what their deaf person might not have had the courage to say. Eve tried to remember all the reasons that could have brought each of her listeners to her at this time and place. Every speech was slightly different, changed by the mood that she somehow sensed of those before her. She wanted to reach everyone and knew it was an impossible dream even as she tried her best to make it a reality. And sometimes, like today, she felt the audience warm in her hands, leaning toward her, absorbing her belief in a future, a strong tomorrow that demanded but gave, too, to those brave enough to step out of their physical and mental cages and into the freedom of their own choices. Her talk lasted an hour, every word a breath of hope and belief. Smiles curled on lips that had forgotten how to lift up in joy. Thoughts that had come to the hall shrouded in gray suddenly found a light source. The closed-minded opened a few doors. Maybe the changes wouldn't last in everyone. There was always that chance. But for this moment, this time, Eve had come and touched the lives of those in need and filled the void with something richer than despair and pain.

ONE

The fire popped and sizzled gently in the hearth while the three nondescript mutts lying before it slept on, aware only of the heat and the man each loved, who sat across the room, his feet propped on an antique desk, beautifully restored. Sloane McGuire glanced up as a particularly loud pop drew his attention from the book he had been reading for most of the evening. His eyes were dark, intense, while his hair, in this light, was only a shade darker. He stared at the fire for a moment, gauging whether he would have to put on another log. He didn't want to break the thread of the story he was reading for the mundane chore. A moment of consideration decided him. He could finish the book before the fire needed replenishing. He looked down at the printed page, readjusted the hardback's position, and continued. The story wasn't new in its format of a single human, losing something very, very precious and yet turning that loss into something positive. Human nature to

11

him was very impressive in all its guises, but this woman, Eve Noble, had done more than just triumph. She had found a key for which he had been searching most of his life. He sensed it in her words, the passion, the dedication, the joy she found in life itself in spite of her deafness.

He closed the book a few minutes later and studied the color picture of the author that graced the back of the dust cover. She didn't look like a fighter, a person who would take up a battle against uneven odds. He studied the green eyes, the straight silky blond hair, the delicate features. She would have made a good model for a storybook princess. He smiled faintly at his poetic turn. Like most of the male population he had learned that a woman's looks were often not the most honest thing about her. The gentlest smile could hide the steel of a conqueror. The softest touch could precede a knife expertly inserted to the core of a man's emotions. The gentle sex had a strength that man could never hope to match and a ruthlessness that could be triggered almost as quickly as the female's loving and compassion.

Sloane looked away from Eve's one-dimensional face and thought of the man who had given him the book. Mark Clemens wanted something from him. He hadn't sent this book with a request to read it for no reason, he decided as he dialed Mark's home. "I finished it," he said when Mark answered on the fourth ring. "Now, why was it so important that I read it tonight?" He gave his littered desk a mild look. He had papers to grade and some recreational reading of his own he had wanted to do. Both could have waited. "I do have other work."

"I know," Mark murmured apologetically. "Before I tell you why, how about telling me what you thought of Eve's story?"

"It was good. Well written. Passionate. Inspiring. Thought provoking," he stated flatly, not prepared to take one thing away from Eve Noble's work and life even to protect himself from whatever favor his friend was seeking. "But you know that. As I recall, this particular work hit a bestseller list and stayed for a while."

Mark ignored the last remark to offer, "How would you like to meet her?"

Sloane hesitated although he did want to meet this woman. Her words had marked him, making him think of things he had not touched in years. She demanded his emotional input in a way few things beyond his family and his work at Beginning Now did. And because he had dealings with the deaf he knew something of her life, the demands and the many obstacles. "Not many thinking people wouldn't like to meet her." He recognized Mark's ploys, having been on the receiving end too many times. "Just get to the point. What do I have to do with Eve Noble?"

"She's coming here to Duke next month to speak. I'm loaning her and her sister the guest house for her stay. And, since neither of them know the area, they'll need a guide. I thought of you."

Sloane frowned faintly. Although his schedule was full this term, he had an able assistant. He could make time, but he still didn't understand why he should. "Why?"

"For the most part, coincidence. The day I received her letter confirming her appearance was the day you were telling me about the day care center and the two kids you have with hearing problems.''

Sloane could feel some undercurrent he didn't recognize in the way Mark kept sliding around his questions. But for the life of him he couldn't think what his friend was planning beyond what he had already admitted. "That's a giant of a leap to tie the two together. Besides, I have classes, in case you've forgotten.''

"You could get your aide to take over for the week. Actually it's a weekend, the week, and the following Saturday.''

Sloane's brows rose at the length of Eve's visit to Duke University. A well-respected alumnus, Mark was on one of the committees that handled the scheduling of speakers, housing for their stay, and guides to the area if needed. Rarely had Duke's hospitality been extended to such a length. "What are you planning?''

"A faculty dinner among other things.''

Sloane groaned. The gathering of his colleagues was not an auspicious occasion in his opinion. Most of them, individually, were interesting people, but collectively they had a tendency to send outsiders into a state of intellectual shock, and him to sleep. "I can already see Professor Mullens at the punch table.''

Mark laughed. "Some things never change. That's one of the reasons I need you. I want Eve to have good memories of her time with us. She's doing us a big favor by speaking on such short notice. She's just come off a demanding tour.''

"I have a feeling that you're leaving something out?"

Mark sighed ruefully. He should have known better than to try to sneak up on Sloane's blind side. He didn't have one. "That picture on the back of her book doesn't do Eve justice. She travels with her sister and she is just as pretty but in a more understated way. I have met them both and I liked them. But neither one of them look as if they could protect themselves from anyone trying to impose on them. I want Eve's stay to go smoothly. It would be nice if we could give back something of what she will be giving us. With your background with those street kids, the way you pick up strays and the like, and the fact that you can sign, I think you would handle Eve's uniqueness without pandering to it. That last, my friend, I think may well be the most important, from what I can tell of the lady. The first time I met Eve, I made the mistake of apologizing for not being able to sign . . . and then capped that gaff off by speaking slowly, as though I were talking to someone lacking in intelligence. The end result is that she let me know, very nicely I might add, that neither effort was needed." Mark grimaced, remembering how awkward he had felt, through his own fault more than hers. "I don't want someone who's likely to make the same kind of stupid mistakes as I did. I know you won't. You have a touch for what hurts other people and you take care to walk gently around anyone's weakness."

Sloane shifted uncomfortably with the accolade. Yes, he noticed the wounds of others. When one is scarred, it is easier to see the same in another.

But what he did wasn't that special. There were many other people in the world doing a lot more. "I'd think a woman would be better suited for escort services."

"I did consider it," Mark admitted honestly. "But Beth thought differently. According to my wife, a woman much prefers a man to another woman for things like eating out, evening engagements, escort duties, et cetera. And Eve's schedule will be loaded with all of that. Plus, you're only three blocks from the guest house. I've had the doorbell rigged with a light, and the phone company is trying to get the special hookup so Eve can read her calls, but that won't solve her problems completely, as you well know."

Sloane sighed, wishing he could put his finger on just what was bothering him about Mark's request. Every reason made sense and both of them knew what Mark had yet to put into words. The woman he had met through her written words was one of those rare people who didn't seem capable of protecting herself from those who would use her. Eve Noble seemed to have an incredible ability to give of herself. And in his world, as in most others, that trait put her at risk. He thought of his colleagues, those who, with the best intentions, would pick her brain. She would need someone beside her to act as buffer. That realization was the decision maker.

"All right." He reached for a pen and paper. "Give me the schedule." Mark was quick to comply, rattling off dates and engagements. "There is a lot of free time in here,'' Sloane observed halfway through the list.

"I know. To be honest, I turned down a few people.''

"Why?''

"She looked tired to me, the kind of exhaustion that marks a person. I almost backed out of asking her to come to us, but I just couldn't forget the power of her writing, the good she could do here.''

"So that's why you're loaning her your guest house and giving her to me.'' Sloane stared at the picture on the dust cover once more. "I'll take care of your speaker,'' he murmured without taking his eyes from Eve's face.

Mark's gratitude was immediate and genuine. "If you have any problems, call. Otherwise, your judgment is the rule.''

Sloane noted the offer absently as he hung up. Eve Noble. She looked like an angel. And her eyes held a light that he had never seen, a kind of serenity that seemed to extend all the way to her soul. He felt such peace in that look. Such acceptance. Maybe it was a trick of a good photographer, but he wanted to believe in that look more than he had wanted anything in a long time. He thought of her writing as his forefinger traced the outline of her delicate bones. There was something intimate in the study of an author's work. So much could be learned that one rarely discovered in the confusion of personal contact. Written words were amazingly clear in their portrayal of values, of needs, hopes, pains, beliefs. Eve Noble had touched him, made him think, wish, and remember. Her power and strength were more

than just an ability to portray emotion on paper. She
had depth. And how often in his life, when he had
looked for and needed that depth in a woman, had
it been lacking? Perhaps, it had been lacking in *him*
somehow. Perhaps he had expected too much. He
didn't know and had finally stopped trying to answer
the frustrating riddle. Life was good, maybe not great
but certainly livable now. He had his work, his project, Beginning Now, and he had his family and
friends. Some would have called his life a lonely one
because of his limited personal life. His father was
definitely not happy that he had shown no hint of
following in his brothers' footsteps and getting himself a wife.

Eve's Madonna smile whispered of so many dreams.
He remembered her written thoughts on children, the
love that had shown in each word, the need for the
special joy of nurturing a baby into adulthood. He
had been interested in her story from the beginning,
but those few sentences had caught him as nothing
ever had in his life. He had wanted to throw the
book away, for it hurt too much to read on. To see
how she spoke of family, values, belief systems, in
ways that anyone could understand and ache to learn
more about, had killed the need to turn from her
intensity. He had held her book in his hands, his
eyes trained on the page to the exclusion of all else.
And when the book was done he knew that no one
would ever reach into his soul and paint pictures of
his lost dreams with so much love, compassion, and
yearning.

Sloane rose and went to the window, remembering
too much and wanting even more. He understood

better than most the word *impossible*. He would have
no family of his own blood. There would be no Eve
in his life ready to give him a child of her body.
Fate had chosen a different path for him. He couldn't
afford futile wishes and dreams. Eve had moved him,
touched his lonely soul. She had given him a gift
that she would never know. He would meet her,
learn more of her, and maybe if the same Fates that
had stolen his future were kind, he would finally find
a measure of peace in his life during the few days
he would share with this extraordinary woman. He
smiled faintly, no humor in the curve of his lips or
the light in his dark eyes. Most men would think of
other things when confronted with the prospect of
time spent with a beautiful woman. Perhaps Mark
had chosen well after all.

"At least she won't have to worry about fending
off unwanted passes," he murmured, unaware that
his dogs had lifted their heads to listen to his slow
drawl. Sloane had eyes only for the darkness of the
night beyond his window. It simply echoed the shadows in his soul. Others might shun the night. He
called it friend.

"I thought you were going to rest after this last
tour." Gay studied her sister as she lightly served
her breakfast plate. The early-morning sun streamed
around her, creating a golden aura that seemed somehow to go with Eve's pale serenity. But that calm
was marred this day by lines of weariness and faint
shadows beneath her eyes. Her appetite wasn't good,
either. Gay worried. The whole family did. Eve had
a way of taking too much on her slender shoulders,

using her strength to the last ounce. She needed a keeper, someone who loved her enough to curb her wish to take the whole world to her breast and soothe the hurts of life.

"I was going to rest." Eve smiled gently as she lifted a cup of tea to her lips. "You're worrying again." She drank sparingly, then put down her cup with a concealed sigh. Gay had on her maternal look. Eve felt the weight of that expression and the love that bolstered it. Her whole family loved her this way, watching over her, always there to catch her if she even looked as though she were going to stumble. No amount of gentle remonstrations had worked, and Eve just couldn't bring herself to hurt them by demanding her independence. So she stayed silent, striving to remember the love rather than the smothering effects that sometimes accompanied it.

"I really am fine. I am tired but not exhausted."

"You will be after these speeches at Duke." Gay leaned forward, knowing by the steady look in Eve's eyes that she was probably wasting her breath trying to make Eve reconsider. "I could feel easier about this if it were just a day or two. But it's more than a week."

Eve smiled faintly. "I think it might be fun. You've been muttering about needing a short vacation away somewhere."

"This isn't it."

"Maybe it is. Think of it. A guest house all our own. A personal guide."

"This Professor McGuire is probably as old as the hills and dry as dust."

Eve laughed, her eyes dancing with mischief. "He could be young and gorgeous."

Gay frowned deeply. "Don't be silly. Mark Clemens wouldn't have done that. I haven't seen a man with his kind of manners in years. He was so careful to assure us of our privacy and that this professor was the pattern of respectability and community service."

Eve nibbled at her scrambled eggs and toast. "You know very well you'll enjoy seeing the University. It has a long history, and it's supposed to be very beautiful."

"I'd much rather poke in some antique shops and flea markets."

"Maybe our professor will be able to find someone to take you or maybe he'll even go himself."

Gay's disgusted look denied that kind of pleasure. "I learned a long time ago not to wish for the moon, you'll only end up with moldy cheese."

Eve shook her head, smiling although she didn't feel like it. Gay's cynicism had not improved over the years they had shared the same house. Eve hated what circumstances and tragedies had created in her gentle, loving sister. Once Gay had more than lived up to her name. Now, she smiled but did not laugh. She hovered around her as though she, Eve, were the only person in the world who gave her life focus. It wasn't right, but as yet Eve hadn't been able to think of a way to help Gay find herself again. So she waited, in the silence of the night, praying for something or someone to touch her sister's heart, to bring alive once again that joyous sense of loving that was uniquely Gay.

"So when exactly do we leave?" Gay asked.

"Next Friday."

Gay sighed and poured herself another cup of coffee. "I'll make a deal with you. I won't keep muttering, as you call it, if you'll laze around the pool until it's time for us to leave."

"You know very well it's going to take both of us to catch up here."

"I'll take care of the small stuff."

Eve recognized Gay's stubborn look. Her deal was just one more example of the cotton batting that went with her deafness. Irritation edged toward anger. But as always she thought of what her family had borne for her sake. Even if she wanted to break out she couldn't forget that. So she swallowed the anger and bent her mind to finding a way of satisfying them both. If she had a prayer for Gay, she had one for herself as well. One day, she would find someone who loved her enough not to wrap her in pretty paper, bound in a ribbon called love and held safe from the world at large. She wanted the joy of walking beside someone who loved her, standing on her own, giving as much as she took, sharing completely all that she was without worrying that she would be hurting her love with her need to be strong.

"We'll do what absolutely must be done and leave the rest until we get back. That way we both can play at the pool."

Gay shook her head. "I don't know why I even try to make you see that you're not superwoman. I never win."

"Is it a deal?"

"You know it is."

"Then let's get started. The sooner begun, the sooner done."

Gay grimaced. "You sound like something out of a quote book."

Eve rose, her dishes in hand. "And you're just irritated that you didn't get your own way." Eve didn't wait to see if there would be a rebuttal. For now, she had won her point. But there would be another day, another small battle for her independence, another compromise out of love.

Sloane leaned against the chain-link fence, feeling the heat of the sun beat down on him. The beginnings of spring were in the air, even here in this rundown section of town, surrounded by buildings that had seen better days and people who had more of a reason to curse than to extend a hand to anyone new in their territory. The lot spread before him was large, nearly three parcels wide. It was no longer a weed- and trash-filled space with nothing to recommend a second look. The weeds were almost gone, the debris cleared away. A new basketball court with its regulation-size surface and bright orange rims on poles at each end took up one part of the whole. Soon there would be a tennis court, small playground, and a soccer field, each with its own fence to guard it from encroachment by the others. Sloane nodded, satisfied for now with what Beginning Now, Inc., was accomplishing. There was still so much to be done, but they were making a good start. Suddenly, a burst of male voices drew his wandering attention. Sloane glanced at the watch on his wrist which kept the official time. He grinned as he started a mental countdown for the last few seconds of the basketball game he was supposed to be refereeing.

"Shoot! Shoot, man!" Grunts, groans, and a number of rather graphic curses muddied the air as ten boys of various ages jostled, elbowed, and, in general, fought for possession of the basketball. The ball sailed through the air, bounced on the edge of the rim of the basket, held there for a second, then dropped in.

Sloane blew the whistle. The teams erupted into a mass of arms and legs, half of the owners celebrating their victory and the other half already demanding a rematch. "I never thought all of you would make it, but you did. One whole game without one man getting tossed out on his butt."

The orange and blue squads turned as one entity to confront Sloane as he joined them. He grinned as he tucked his hands into his pockets and shifted his weight into a lazy, slouching stance. He had started with only three kids and now he had reached two full teams. There were still a lot of holdouts on the street, but he and Beginning Now were starting to win this small war against poverty, drugs, and governmental bureaucracy.

"It's those damn penalties, coach," Bonzo, the smallest guy on the orange team, explained. He was the talker, the clown.

Five or six heads nodded agreement while every expression showed disgust at the work they had had to do around the youth center as a repayment for every infraction on the court. Being tossed out cost a whole day, usually working in the lot, clearing debris and weeds under the coach's too-vigilant eyes.

"Remember, you promised us a reward if we went one whole game without a man being thrown out," Bonzo reminded Sloane, again speaking for the whole group.

Fighting a laugh, Sloane inclined his head. "I did. It's in the rec hall." He felt them watching him as he started for the newly painted two-story building one of the top developers in Durham had donated in this run-down section of town. The whole neighborhood was still reeling over discovering that soon they would have not only the large lot with its limited team play facilities, the building with its maze of rooms for meetings and other activities, but a daycare center and a big room at the back for the teens to gather, play their music, and just plain hang out, as well. Almost everyone had been suspicious at first. But in the six months of occupation, Beginning Now, Inc. had proven it wasn't just another bunch of do-gooders with more stupid ideas than practical help for those who had need of almost every necessity of life.

"You going to tell us what we won?" Crazy asked gruffly, the first one to follow, even though he had been the last to join.

Sloane didn't stop walking, but he did glance at Crazy. He read and understood the challenge in the younger boy's eyes. Crazy wanted to be disappointed. He didn't believe in Sloane or his promises and he wanted to prove it to his friends before they were hurt as he must have been hurt too many times. "Talk is easy. I'd rather show you."

Crazy glared at him, his eyes even more suspicious. "Probably something stupid, anyway."

Sloane opened the back door to the building and led the way down the hall with Crazy matching his steps. "It might be, I suppose, but I don't think it is." He stopped at the doorway of the huge room at the rear of the first floor. This was the area that he had set aside for the younger adults. It was a place free of drugs, danger from being on the street, and the one place they could truly claim as their own.

The group fanned out around him, peering into the room, their voices slowly dying away as they saw the objects taking up space. "Hot damn!"

Sloane didn't recognize the voice that spoke, but he heard the sheer amazement and grinned, his eyes lighting with satisfaction although he said nothing. This was a game that he had learned to play through trial and error. Pushing these kids, demanding even the simplest of human emotions, was the quickest way he had found to lose them. So he waited. Patience had always been one of his greatest strengths and through Beginning Now it had grown even stronger.

"A pool table," Bonzo muttered as though he couldn't believe it. He pushed past Sloane and Crazy to head for the largest of the surprises. "A new pool table."

Slowly, the teams moved into the room, spreading out to circle the table. A light hung suspended over the center of the green felt surface, a rack of cues hung on the wall. Sloane stood on the fringe of the gathering, not intruding. For a moment he wished his brother Stryker and his wife Tempest could have been there to see what their gift meant to these kids. His friends and family had been more than generous with his brainchild. Mike had supplied the flooring for the whole building while Slater and Stryker had chipped in for the paint and building materials to bring the structure up to code. Joshua Luck's company had donated the money to buy the adjacent lot and set up the courts and equipment.

"You might want to look under those sheets against the wall," Sloane murmured when no one seemed to notice that there were more new additions in the room besides the pool table.

Crazy stared at Sloane across the width of the table as Bonzo and his brother investigated the sheet-swathed squares. Two new video games, courtesy of Alex and Lorelei Kane, stood revealed to a ragged chorus of murmured appreciation. "What do you want from us, man?" Crazy demanded, disbelief and frustration in his eyes.

Sloane faced the oldest of the boys, realizing that the confrontation he had always known waited in the future had finally come. "You won't believe me if I tell you. But it's nothing. I don't want one damn thing."

Crazy's mouth formed a sneer that sat too easily on a face made too old with its experience. "Right. Tell it to a fool. Not me."

Sloane hated the cynicism he saw in Crazy's eyes, but only time and patience would change him if it could be done at all. "What could I want?"

"Hell, I don't know." Crazy shrugged angrily. He could feel his friends watching, waiting. He knew gifts were never freely given.

Sloane pulled his hands out of his pockets and held them palms-up. "No strings. You can come and use this stuff. You can even help your friends steal it if that's the kind of thing you do. You can rip it up or take care of it. There are no guards here, no alarms. From where I'm sitting, I'd say that makes me and the organization more in your power than you are in ours."

Crazy stared hard at him, the blunt words doing more than any number of softer reasons might have. He hadn't thought of the situation in that light. He and his friends did have the power. He glanced down at the pool table, then at the video games his little brother would love. His sister was even now in the day-care room down the hall while his mother worked. They ate good here, better than at home, and he didn't even mind the work to clean up the outside, although he wasn't about to admit that to his friends. He looked back at Sloane, respecting the big man in spite of himself. There was something to depend on in his eyes. Crazy lived by his instincts, survived by them. He knew when he could trust and when he couldn't. He didn't have to believe everything he was told, but he could play a wait-and-see game.

"It won't get stolen," he muttered finally, coming as close as he intended to admitting he helped out at home by "finding things" on the street. "Or messed up."

Sloane inclined his head once, reading the admission accurately. One more start in a long list of needs to be met. "Fair enough." He walked to the cue rack and hefted a stick. "How about a game?"

Crazy's eyes narrowed. "You want to get beat?"

Sloane grinned, his eyes flashing with male challenge accepted. "You can try," he invited pleasantly.

TWO

Sloane rotated his neck wearily as he drove home. It had been a long day with classes in the morning at the University and then the rest of the afternoon at Beginning Now. There was still more work on his agenda for the evening, papers to mark, and calls to his pool of benefactors for a few more amenities at the center. He would be lucky if he saw his bed before midnight. Not that it really mattered because there was only himself whom he had to please. He glanced around, appreciating the beauty of the state he had made his home. The hills of the tri-city area of Raleigh, Durham, and Chapel Hill, North Carolina, were pretty in the spring. The temperature was cool enough to nip at the skin and the trees still hadn't filled out completely, but the promise of the earth's renewal was clear in every bud, every ray of sunshine. He liked this time of year, perhaps more than most seasons, although each had its own appeal. He thought of his house, empty with the exception of his dogs, mutts rescued from the local pound. His lame ducks, his strays, as his father and brothers would say. He smiled faintly at the thought. He had filled his life with the wounded, the damaged. He made no apology for his choices, accepting them as he accepted all things that came and went with time.

He eased up the incline of his drive and into the garage attached to the natural stone house that was the same multicolored rock of which the original buildings of Duke University were constructed. The soft grays, reds, and creams blended into the surrounding trees and evergreens and the gentle contours of the hills around the school and his neighborhood. The land was silent, almost reverent in its attention to the sound of man and the creatures of the earth and the sky. The setting was picture-postcard beautiful, but more than that, it was home. Sloane understood that word, had longed for it in his youth with the intensity that only the young can give to impossible wishes. But his hadn't stayed an impossible wish. As soon as he had had the ordering of his own life, he had created a base, this place that looked as if it had stood against the hand of nature and man for a very long time. Age was a graceful cloak and the trees that sheltered his house a protection from the eyes of those who would pry into his life. He liked his privacy, although he wasn't rabid on the subject. Occasionally he had friends over, but these days most of his time was spent standing in front of his classes or fighting the multitentacled beast called poverty, hidden from view of those he sought to aid by the corporate entity of Beginning Now.

Sloane entered through the kitchen at the back of

the house. The dogs were curled up in one corner of the room and only raised their heads at his entrance. Three tails wagged, but not one body moved from the combined heat of three to greet him. He laughed, the sound filling the silent kitchen with life. That stirred some energy into lazy bones. Goof, the largest, got to his feet, stumbled his way to Sloane's side, and jammed his huge head into Sloane's thigh with enough force to stagger them both. Sloane braced against the clumsiness that no amount of maturing had improved and patted the wiry fur.

"Never mind, old son. Clumsy or not, you still have character."

Goof grunted his imitation of a dog. Sloane shook his head as he reached for the coffeepot he always kept plugged in on a timer. After pouring himself a cup, he left the room and headed for the back of the house where his study was located. No fire burned in the grate today. Neither the warmth nor the light was needed. He sat down at his desk, glancing idly at the papers he had to mark before the weekend was over. This was his last free weekend before Eve and her sister arrived. Because he wanted to hand his aide a clean slate, he was going to be very busy. He had already set up in detail the ground he wanted covered. The class had the syllabus he had handed out at the beginning of the year. Helen could handle the schedule for the week of Eve's visit. Suddenly the sound of a vehicle door slamming caught his attention. Less than a minute later the doorbell rang with a distinctive rhythm.

His plans put on mental hold, Sloane strolled to the door, reaching and opening it just in time to stop another attack on his ears. "Leave the doorbell on, Mike," he commanded, grinning at the older version of his own face.

Mike's grin matched his son's. No one could have mistaken the kinship, for the McGuire genes bred true and strong in all its offspring. "Took you long enough. You got company?"

"No, I don't have company." Ignoring his father's hastily concealed disappointment, he stepped back so his Mike could enter. "Are you visiting or just passing through?"

"Well, that kind of depends on you, son." Mike eyed the cup in Sloane's hand. "Tell me you have some more of that going. There's a nasty little nip in the air for a man who has just spent a couple of weeks in the hot sun of Texas."

Sloane gestured him toward the kitchen. "It's on the counter." He followed Mike's broad back down the hall. "How are Stryker and Tempest?" The oldest of Sloane's brothers lived with his wife Tempest in Houston.

"Don't ask. Only Stryker could deal with that crazy woman at a time like this." Mike poured himself a mug, then turned, a frown killing his smile. "You know what that daredevil wants to do? She wants to have her first baby in their bed, without any doctor and nothing to help her if something goes wrong."

Big hands wrapped around the mug, clenching at memories that time hadn't done anything to destroy. He had lost his wife in childbirth. God had spared his perfect, triplet sons, but He had called home Mike's young bride and destroyed the future he had taken for granted with the intensity and commitment of a strong, young heart bent on carving a niche for himself and his wife. The thought of that kind of thing happening to any of his three boys was more than he could handle.

"I had to leave. Stryker kept telling me not to worry about anything, but I knew if I stayed I'd stick my big mouth in where it doesn't belong. A man and his woman deserve their privacy." He took a sip of the dark liquid and glared at Sloane. "I don't understand that girl."

Sloane heard the worry lacing his father's voice and felt for the older man. "No, but Stryker does, and if he says don't worry, then you can take his word to the bank," he replied, looking him straight in the eye. Soft words had never been the McGuire way. "Neither Tempest nor Joy is an ordinary woman. You wouldn't have wanted either for Stryker or Slater."

"Or for you."

Sloane shook his head. "Don't start, Mike. I'm not them and I don't want to be. I've had my shots at the marriage line and I haven't managed to even make it to the altar. I'm tired of trying."

Mike scowled. It was one of his best expressions and usually had the object of that look ready to run. But not Sloane. "McGuires don't quit. Besides, you don't want to be alone all your life, son."

"It's worked for you."

"I've had my boys."

They had this argument so often that Sloane felt as though he were reciting dialogue learned by rote.

"You could have remarried. I know damn well you've had the opportunity."

Mike shrugged, angling for a new opening to talk to Sloane about his bachelor status. The days he had spent with Stryker and Tempest had made him more determined than ever to try to reach Sloane. "Maybe. But a man has responsibilities. I didn't want you three to pay tolls on my choices. I'd lost your mother and there was no guarantee that any stepmother I might bring home would take to handling my trio of devils."

Sloane grinned, his eyes lighting with memories. "Two devils. Stryker and Slater were the ones always in trouble."

Mike grunted, his lips twitching in spite of himself. "Yeah, they were the ones I usually caught, but I've learned a thing or two since you've grown up. You always get what you want and you rarely head after whatever it is in a way that can be traced. You are a very subtle man. I missed that when I was raising you. None of the rest of us has that trait. Must be your mother in you," he added, trying to call to mind the young girl he had loved so much all those years ago. "Of the three of you, you're the one I wouldn't like to face on the opposite side of any fence. I'm not sure I would win."

Surprised at the assessment, Sloane didn't say anything for a moment. "For a compliment like that, I guess I could spring for pizzas tonight," he suggested finally, changing the course of the conversation.

Mike's look said he recognized the tangent but would allow it in the interests of keeping peace. Both men chuckled. Mike clapped the middle of his triplets on the back. "Son, that was no compliment. It was the truth."

"You look as though you're pleased with your world. What's up?" Pippa Luck dropped into her husband's lap and wound her arms around his neck. Her pale eyes glittered with amusement and the passion that always smoldered whenever she was within range of Josh's lean body.

"You'd be pleased, too, if you had just pulled off what I did." Josh nuzzled his wife's slender neck, kissing her just below the ear. The responsive shiver through her delicate body brought a wicked glint to his eyes as he raised his head.

"Don't look at me like that. At least not until after you tell me the reason for that smug expression I saw on your face when I came in." Even as she verbally denied the desire slowly coming to life between them, her hands were busy tracing well-learned patterns of sensations over his skin.

"Do you remember how you've been complaining about not being able to think of one female of our acquaintance who would do for Sloane McGuire?"

Pippa stopped in midstroke, her eyes narrowing with his I-know-something-you-don't-know tone. "I remember."

Josh grinned at her expression, enjoying the sensation of having put one over on his usually ahead-of-any-game spouse. "Well . . ." He drew the word out for maximum effect.

Pippa's glare intensified. "Do you know I don't

think I've exhausted my bag of tricks even after all these years?''

Long experience with Pippa had given Josh the edge he hadn't possessed in the early days of their marriage. Now, he was a match for his fiery-natured mate and all the intriguing twists of her truly unique mind. "Want to demonstrate?"

Tipping back her head, exposing the pure line of her throat, Pippa laughed deeply, the husky sound arousing even in its delight. "No, you rotten male. I do not want to demonstrate. I want a certain man I know to stop teasing me and tell me what's going on.''

"I have found a possible match for Sloane," he announced with all the pomp of an MC presenting the top act to an exclusive audience.

Pippa stared at him, her humor taking a nose-dive into suspicion. "What do you mean you've found a match? You've spent years deploring my matchmaking and then you calmly announce you've done the same thing yourself.''

"I figured since I couldn't get you to see reason, I'd join you in the fun. And it has been fun," he admitted with a grin that was every bit as wicked as any of Pippa's at her best. "It has also been one long list of frustration and work. I had no idea how hard it would be to get two people from different areas of the country into the same geographic range without telling the parties involved. On top of that there is a second woman in the pot to stir up the situation. I had to find a way to amuse her or I might have set the scene for the wrong person at the wrong time.''

Pippa's eyes widened at the last bit of information. Josh tapped her chin with his finger, grinning in delight at her dumbfounded look. "Gotcha."

"Who is it?" Pippa asked finally, promising herself she'd wait to hear the rest before she exploded.

"Now, *that* I think I'll keep a secret," her spouse decided with no nice intent.

Pippa touched his face, for the first time worried about her avocation being practiced by someone else, even if that someone was the man she loved above all others. "Josh, this isn't a game. Someone could get hurt."

He nodded calmly, watching her closely. "I think I've heard that before."

"You can't . . ." Pippa paused, looking more carefully at Josh's expression. The waiting quality warned her. She touched his face, realizing that she had almost made a serious error. "Just for a second, I nearly accused you of trying to teach me a lesson."

"What stopped you?"

"Trust. Love. And knowing you. You wouldn't put someone's life in jeopardy just to show me what you were afraid would happen if one of my little arrangements came apart."

"No, I wouldn't," he agreed, kissing her once, hard enough to convey his relief at her assessment. "I meant what I said. I wanted to share this with you and I've changed my mind about what you do. When I look around at all the people you have brought together, I can't remember why I thought my narrow-minded view was best. I didn't plan to involve myself in Sloane's life as an example. That only occurred to me as I did. I really do think this woman will be wonderful for him.''

Pippa cuddled closer to his warmth, smiling at his earnest look. ''Now that we have that settled, you can tell me who she is.''

''Nothing doing. This is my secret and I'm going to hug it as long as I can, but you're welcome to wear yourself out trying to guess.''

''That's not nice.'' Pippa nuzzled his ear, her tongue expertly tracing the shape so that maximum sensation was achieved.

''I know.''

Her mouth edged closer to the neck of his shirt, her tongue darting under the fabric in teasing forays. ''Complacency is not a pleasant trait in one's mate.''

''No.'' Josh cleared his throat before he continued. ''It's damned infuriating.''

Her fingers opened the first two buttons. She could feel the hard thrust of his body against her thighs. ''Voice of experience, is it?''

Josh caught her hips, pulling her tight against him. He looked her straight in the eye as he let her feel the full extent of his need, the need she had been fueling since the moment she had walked into his study. ''I hope you locked the door.''

''I thought you had work to do.''

He laughed huskily. ''I do. Husbandly work. It might just take most of my energy and most of the day.'' He pulled the rainbow-hued scarf she had wrapped around her upper body to create a kind of scanty-top affair. The effect on a woman with Pippa's lush endowments was decidedly erotic. ''I hope you remembered to turn your computer off," he whispered against her scented flesh as he teased first one nipple then the other.

Pippa tipped back her head, her lashes closing as any thought to the chapter she had left half-finished fled. "I'll worry about that later," she murmured throatily, her fingers sliding through the silvered strands of his hair.

"I do like your thinking, love of mine," he said, rising with her in his arms. He walked with her to the couch, laying her down on her side before stretching out beside her. He traced the fullness of one breast without taking his eyes from his wife's face. Her fifty years sat gently on her shoulders and because of her, on his. She had given him more than her body. She had taught him how to live each moment to the last drop. And she had shown him how to include others in their happiness. What she had done for Lyla and Joe, Diana and Jason, Lorelei and Alex, Rich and Christiana, Stryker and Tempest, and Slater and Joy, had touched him in spite of his protests. He could no more watch someone suffer the pain of loneliness and aching emptiness than he could watch one of his children hurt. Of the McGuire triplets, Sloane had held Josh's interest more than the others. He had seen in Sloane some of his own dammed-up emotions, walls, and needs carefully concealed in a full life. And because of a fluke of events, he had been privy to something that Sloane had told no one else. That something was the root of Sloane's narrow life. Josh had ached for him, but until he had remembered a certain very special woman, the daughter of a business associate, he hadn't known what could be done. Now he had set the wheels of Fate in motion. The meeting was arranged. The players on their marks. All he could do was cross his fingers and pray.

THREE

"I can't believe the plane was early. Planes are never early," Gay said as she looked at her watch. All around them people were getting to their feet to collect their belongings before they filled the aisle as they hurried to deplane. The noise rose with the activity as the seats began to empty.

Eve watched her fellow passengers leave. Families were her favorite of all travelers, especially the children. They had such an appreciation for what others took for granted. She smiled faintly as one little girl darted down the crowded corridor toward them, leaving her mother, carrying her little brother, behind. The mother called her daughter's name. Eve read the anxiety in the other woman's face and reached out a hand to stop the child.

"Honey, I'd wait for Mom. You might get lost," she said gently, smiling into the dark-brown eyes trained so curiously on her face.

"You talk funny," the girl said with youthful frankness.

Eve's lips quivered as she restrained a grin when she read the words. "I know."

"How come?"

The mother joined them, eyeing Eve suspiciously as she took her daughter's hand. "I'm sorry she bothered you," the mother apologized, tucking the child closely to her side.

"She was no bother." Her gaze moved to the baby in the older woman's arms. "You have lovely children."

The woman glanced down at the sleeping infant, then moved aside for the last person to pass. "Thank you," she murmured, warming slightly. Then she smiled faintly. "Thank you for stopping her, too. I was terrified she'd get away from me in this mess."

"A crowd makes it easy to lose someone." Eve rose, noticing the diaper bag dangling from the woman's shoulder and a clear plastic carrier of toys for the little girl, along with a purse and a sweater. "My sister and I don't have any carry-on luggage. Could we help you with some of that?"

"I couldn't let you."

Eve grinned, recognizing the need and the lingering suspicion. "I promise the minute we get to a place with someone else to help you, Gay and I will be on our way."

The woman's face reddened, then she laughed. "I keep forgetting how nice people can be in the South. Things like this don't usually happen in the city."

Eve eased the diaper bag off her shoulder and put it on her own. Gay took the toy carrier and the sweater.

"My name is Annie," the girl offered, yanking

her hand out of her mother's and thrusting it at Eve. "What's yours?"

"Eve. And this is my sister, Gay."

The dark head tipped as she studied Gay. "She doesn't talk much."

Even laughed. "That's because I don't give her much of a chance." From the corner of her eye she noted the mother relaxing with every word.

Gay touched the younger woman's arm. "Eve's a bit of a Pied Piper with children."

"I see that. She must have some of her own." She shifted her child to a more comfortable position. "Since my daughter's getting names, mine's Lisa."

"She's a pretty child." Gay motioned the woman to precede her as they followed Eve and Annie.

"Are you here on a visit?" Lisa asked, speaking to Eve's back.

Gay shook her head. "She can't hear you. My sister's deaf."

Lisa stopped in the middle of the aisle. "You're kidding. But she speaks like she can hear us."

"Eve is lip reading. She's very good at it," Gay said, doing her best to keep the irritation out of her voice. Eve wouldn't like to know that she had hurt this care-worn mother in her defense. She glanced to the pair reaching the exit. "We'd better hurry or we'll lose them."

"That's terrible." Lisa looked at Eve as she chatted with Annie. "But you can't tell."

"It doesn't usually show," Gay murmured.

"But she speaks so well. I thought deaf people sounded odd and that they had to do sign language or something."

Gay mentally winced at Lisa's continued curiosity. Such questions didn't seem to bother Eve, but Gay had never gotten over wanting to tell the curious to stop probing. Eve wasn't a freak to be stared at. She was a functioning woman with all the feelings that went with that role. She controlled her anger, knowing it served no purpose. Lisa's reaction was typical.

The four of them made their way to the gate area. Lisa looked around for her aunt, who was supposed to meet them. "I don't know where she can be. I'd take a taxi, but if I did, my aunt would get here!" She turned away from her scrutiny of the waiting area. "Are you being met?" she asked Eve, speaking loudly and distinctly. Not wanting to be caught staring, her eyes slid away from Eve's face.

Eve looked at Gay, realizing that her sister had told the woman of her deafness. She shook her head slightly, seeing the temper that seemed only to stir for her protection in Gay's eyes. "Yes, but like yours, it seems that our ride is late." She gestured toward the bank of chairs across the room. "We could wait over there."

Lisa nodded jerkily and grabbed Annie's hand. Eve understood the reaction, accepted the sting of what she usually received as a response. She missed the warmth of Annie's small hand tucked in hers. The four, now distinctly separate, moved to the chairs. Annie eyed her mother with a frown, but before she could question the sudden change she sensed but didn't understand, Lisa took her toy bag from Gay and dropped it in her daughter's lap.

Gay grimaced at the blatant ploy. Placing herself between Eve and the two chairs that Lisa had left empty beside them, she sat down. "Some people have no sense," she signed to Eve.

Eve touched her arm, shaking her head. "I'm fine," she signed back. "And you know she doesn't mean to be cruel."

Her hands moved in short choppy motions. "That doesn't make it better."

Eve looked past Gay to Annie's face. "Stop fighting what can't be changed. Think of the future. It's in that child's face, her mind, her words. Tomorrow does come and, with it, changes."

"You forgive too easily."

"And you don't forget at all. Memories only have the right to hurt us if we give them that power."

Gay's hands stilled at the quick return. Before she could find a suitable reply, Annie's voice caught her attention.

"There's Aunt Nellie," she cried, bouncing out of her seat, sending her toys scattering. Her brother awoke with a wail. Her mother called to Annie to stop. Heads turned. Eve half rose as Annie barreled straight through the crowd between her and her relative.

She saw Annie collide with a tall man, bounce back hard enough to land in a hurtful plop on the floor. Before gravity could win its battle with the little girl's balance, two strong hands reached out, wrapped around delicate shoulders, and beat the forces of nature. Annie looked up at her rescuer and gave him a wide, gapped-tooth smile.

Eve, also, studied Annie's protector. He was a handsome man with the kind of face that a child or a woman could trust on sight. He stood a head above most of the others in the room and with his dark hair and eyes, he could easily have been Annie's father. Even the tenderness of his expression as he spoke to the little girl told of caring. Startled at the depth of emotion in his eyes, the gentle smile on his lips, Eve found herself studying him with a degree of concentration she had never given another man. She watched his lips move, each word distinct in her mind. She saw Annie's giggle and traced the child's humor as it journeyed to the man's mouth. His grin was a heartbreaker. She inhaled softly, feeling that smile slide into her heart, touching her in a way she had never experienced. Surprise held her eyes focused on his face beyond the time of simple curiosity. Her gaze narrowed as she examined the effect this stranger could induce. She felt odd, caught in a strange emotional warp. She wanted to touch him, to watch his mouth form words for her. She wanted to see his smile and know that it lived for her. Surprise turned to shock. She did not fantasize. She did not stare. She did not ache for a man's touch. She did not get turned on by a look.

He raised his head. The did nots fled. And she found a new truth as she looked into those dark-chocolate eyes. For one moment, she looked past the barriers that most people weren't even aware of and saw to his soul. Pain. A bleak desert so arid in its emptiness that she mentally reeled from that one glimpse. Her hand lifted fractionally from her side. Her foot rose to take that first step to touch him. Then as swiftly as the link had been forged between them, the emotions slipped into hiding. Shadows, so very many shadows. Although his hands still cradled the child, he seemed somehow to have moved a hundred miles away from any human contact.

Eve was past surprise as she glanced at Annie. He released Annie at the same moment and turned to the older man at his side. Eve watched them speak, then nod in her direction. Even as the pair came toward them and Annie scurried off to meet her aunt, Eve guessed who the man at his side was. Professor Sloane McGuire. Annie's rescuer was probably an aide.

"This must be them," Gay signed.

Eve nodded once, then turned her attention back to the approaching men. She searched the aide's face, trying to find some sign of the man she had seen a few seconds before. He wasn't there. Only a hint of curiosity showed, interest but no more. No pain. No arid desert of need unfulfilled. Eve controlled a shiver. She had never seen such a transformation so quickly achieved. The control needed had to be monumental. Intrigued, she almost missed the introduction and the realization that the 'aide' was none other than Professor Sloane McGuire himself. She stared into his dark eyes as his hand wrapped around hers.

"I should know better than to make quick assumptions," Eve managed. "I thought your father was the professor."

Mike chuckled, blatantly delighted with the mistake. Sloane ignored the sound to focus on the woman. Her photograph had not done her justice. Her hand was small in his, her head coming no higher than his heart. He had thought to be interested in the woman who had risen like a phoenix from the ashes of what could have destroyed another less strong than she. Somehow in the days since he had read that book, he had convinced himself that all the values and dreams that Eve had held dear, all those things he knew were forever beyond his reach, had been the main reason his response to her written words had been so immediate, so complete. He had been wrong. As he held her hand in his, he forgot the peace he had seen in the eyes of her photograph. He remembered instead that second when he had felt her gaze whispering across a crowded room. She had caught him at his most vulnerable, seeing things that he permitted no one to know. In those few instants she had touched him, warming the cold of an emptiness that would never be filled.

Danger! More than a word. A woman. Eve. Survival demanded retreat, mental by necessity but no less effective for all its limits. He released her hand, ignoring the coolness where once her heat had lived.

"You just made his day," he replied calmly as his gaze slipped to the silent woman at Eve's side. "If you have your baggage tickets, I'll collect your luggage while Mike shows you to the car."

Eve couldn't hear the tone he used, but she could certainly sense withdrawal. His features were taut beneath the polite mask that overlay the whole. His body was tense. Mentally, she drew back, protecting herself in the only way open to her. Mark had assured her that Sloane was familiar with the deaf and that he could sign. She had taken the older man at his word. But faced with Sloane and the barrier he had erected made her doubt Mark's words. His reaction to her was considerably more subtle than Lisa's but no less telling. Until she knew for certain what was causing the distance that had been put between them, she would respect that need to turn away. But it hurt, more than it had in a long time, she admitted silently as she reached for the handbag that hung over her shoulder, welcoming the chance to look away while she pulled herself together.

"Here they are," she murmured as she found the tickets and thrust them in Sloane's direction. Without looking at him again, she turned to Mike. The father was an easier proposition than the son. There were no barriers here. Good humor and strength shone in eyes as dark as his son's without the shadows. "We're ready whenever you are."

Mike held out an arm to each of them. "I know that this kind of thing is supposed to be out of fashion, but I would really like to strut through this terminal with two good-looking young ladies at my side." His grin was wicked, the lady-killer expression that had earned him a number of longing sighs from the female population over the years.

Eve laughed. She couldn't help it when his words were accompanied with such a sparkle of mischief. She tucked her hand in the crook of his elbow. "I think I like you, Mike McGuire." She glanced at Gay, surprised to see an expression of merriment on her usually serious sister's face.

"Make that two," Gay added, touched despite herself.

Sloane watched as Mike led the pair away, envying his father in a way he never had. He had courted Eve's smile and won it, basking in its warmth and leaving Sloane to face the cold of her absence. He shook his head, as angry with his thinking as his reactions. She was just a woman, more beautiful than most, gentler than average. The reading of her book, the sharing of the thoughts and emotions that had gone into the telling of her story, had given him an intimate look into her mind. In many ways more intimate than lovemaking would have been. But that knowledge was all on his side. It was seduction of his senses, and he had to remember the danger. He wanted only one thing from Eve Noble—the key to her inner peace. He needed that and that alone. Everything else was just a case of lonely man and lovely woman.

Sloane drove the car, aware of every breath Eve drew as she sat silently beside him. He glanced at her occasionally, ready to point out anything of interest that might catch her eye, but she seemed oblivious to anything around her. Somehow, since he had left her in the terminal, she had locked him out. He wanted to ask her what was wrong, but with his audience, lost though they were in conversation, he didn't dare. So he sat listening with one-quarter attention to the conversation going on behind him. At least Mike didn't seem to be having any trouble with the other half of the Noble pair.

"There's another one," Gay exclaimed, staring out the backseat window. "I can't believe how many antique shops there are around here."

"And garage sales and flea markets," Mike added, eyeing her speculatively.

Gay glanced at him, unable to hide her surprise

and delight at the possibility of another enthusiast. "Do you mean it?"

Mike's face held a similar eagerness. "I think I've found a woman after my own heart. Tell me you like poking around in dusty corners looking at things like saltcellars."

Her smile widened. "And alphabet plates."

"Old tools."

"Cracked crockery."

"Victorian fly traps."

That stopped the list. "That's a new one on me. What is it?"

"The only one I've ever seen was in a museum and it was a blown crystal bottle with a tiny pitcherlike end and a small opening with a top. The fly would enter through the hole to get to the bottom of the bottle where some sweet liquid like syrup or honey lay to tempt him. Once he was in, he couldn't get out again. When you were ready, you opened the larger hole and cleaned the bottle."

"Ingenious."

He grinned. "I thought so. I've been looking for one like it ever since, but I've never found another one."

"At least you knew it existed."

Mike hesitated, then shrugged. "I don't suppose you'd like to go antique hunting with me while you're here? Sloane won't touch those kinds of places. And it isn't nearly as much fun by myself."

Gay searched his face for a moment. He was serious. He really did like treasure hunting in the past. "I'd like that," she said finally. The second pleasure lit his eyes, she added hastily, "As long as Eve doesn't need me." Before Mike could respond, she leaned forward and touched Eve's shoulder.

Eve turned, glad of any diversion to break the silence that had lain between her and Sloane since he had started the car. She had considered turning in her seat to talk to Gay but had finally decided she would take her cue from Sloane.

"Mike was just telling me there are a number of antique places in the area. He likes to poke around in them, too."

Eve glanced at the older man, finding him watching her with something like a challenge in his eyes. "And you want to go along," Eve guessed, knowing her sister's passion for the past.

Gay laughed. "You know I do. I can't drag you into that kind of place." She sobered. "I know we have a lot of things to do, but I thought maybe a couple of hours would be all right."

Eve concealed a sigh. She wanted to assure Gay that she didn't need her to baby-sit every moment, but she couldn't bring herself to hurt her sister. Gay had appointed herself her sister's keeper too many years ago to count. And for a while she had desperately needed to be needed. Eve hadn't minded then. But lately, she had begun to realize that Gay used her as an excuse for not living life to the fullest.

Gay frowned when Eve didn't answer immediately. "I won't go."

Sloane shifted, surprised to discover he didn't like the implication that Eve wouldn't be all right with him. Or if it came to that, on her own. The woman he had read about was far from helpless and the reality he had met was just as strong.

Eve shook her head, irritated at herself for putting the idea into Gay's head. "You definitely have to go. Just make sure you take your credit cards. The last time you went exploring you were broke when we got home," Eve said, using the memory to divert her sister.

Gay's face cleared. She grinned, looking years younger. "But did I ever have a good time."

"What did you get?" Mike demanded.

Eve groaned. "I don't know that even she remembers. We were opening boxes for a week afterward."

Gay gave her a mock glare. "That's a lie." She turned a shoulder to Eve, spoiling the effect with a grin. "Let me see."

Eve watched her sister and Mike for a second, startled at the animation in Gay's face. Eve faced forward again, sighing in satisfaction. The trip was showing some very nice side benefits. Now if her guide would just lighten up.

Eve glanced at Sloane. She'd had enough of the cold shoulder. "Are you going to tell me what's wrong?"

A stoplight caught him, denying him the opportunity to slow his reply. He turned so she could lip-read. "I don't know what you're talking about."

Eve wasn't easily put off. If she had to work with this man for the next week, she didn't intend to do it in silence. "I wouldn't have said you were a liar."

The rebuttal was a surprise. But then again it wasn't. He should have remembered the tenacity she had shown him in the revelation of the obstacles she had surmounted. This was not a woman who understood the word *quit*. He should have been annoyed. Instead, he was intrigued enough to see what she would do next. Sloane looked at her for a moment then said mildly, "You don't know me well enough to have said anything."

"I guess now I'm supposed to retreat to my corner and feel guilty."

The fat-chance tone made his lips twitch despite his determination to keep his interest purely academic. "It would have been nice," he said under his breath.

But Eve's special way of hearing allowed her to thwart him even in that tactic. "I would have said *convenient* is more what you're striving for. I want to know why."

Sloane sighed and surrendered to the woman who had shown him such character in her writing, passion that had imbued every word, the determination, the need to reach out even when the hand was in danger of being knocked away. The very things he had admired about her life and her writing were the very things that held him now against his will. He should have been angry. He wanted to be. But looking into her eyes, he gave up that idea for the duration of her stay. To learn her inner secrets he would have to let her close. For every wall he threw up, she was strong enough to match him brick for brick. Tearing down those barriers would hurt them both, and that was the last thing he wanted for her. She had seen enough pain in her life, lost enough. *He* would not be the cause of her losing anything because of him.

"How about putting my manners down to a bad mood that has nothing to do with you." He hadn't known he was capable of lying.

Eve tipped her head, studying him. "All right. I'll take that because I *don't* know you all that well and it might be the truth, even though I don't think it is." Only the tightening of his fingers on the wheel gave any indication that her words had hit too close to the mark.

"Would you like to rest when you get to the house or do you want to see some of the area?" His role as her guide and escort demanded the question. His needs as a man commanded the words for a break they both could use. He turned down the street toward his destination.

Eve accepted the change of subject. "I would rather see some of the area."

Sloane caught the sudden cessation of conversation in the backseat which Eve wouldn't hear. He glanced in the rearview mirror to see the disapproval on Gay's face. Frowning, his brows rose at the expression.

"We had to get up very early to catch the plane this morning. I don't think sightseeing for Eve is a good idea. This last tour took a lot out of her and she needs her rest," Gay said quickly, the words tumbling out before Eve could realize what she was doing.

Sloane didn't have the luxury of having Eve's back to him so that he could reply. For the second time, Gay had implied that Eve couldn't take care of herself. Anger was too easy. He could see the love and concern in the older woman's face but that didn't make the devaluation of the woman at his side any easier to take. "Do you like surprises?" he asked with one last look at Gay. His head was angled enough for Eve to read his words easily.

Eve smiled, her eyes lighting with enthusiasm. "Love them."

He couldn't resist that eagerness, didn't even want to. He cast a quick look over her clothes. They were a little too nice for where he intended to take her. "You'll need to change into something comfortable and something you won't mind getting dirty if it comes to that."

Intrigued at the mystery, Eve slipped out on her side of the car, barely noticing the gracious home that Mark Clemens had put at her disposal for the duration of her stay at Duke. "Don't I get any more clues?" she demanded.

"No." He came around to her side of the car, chuckling at her disgusted look. "That would spoil the surprise."

Mike joined his son. "I'll get the luggage, Sloane, while you show the ladies the house." He took the keys from Sloane.

A few minutes later, Mike and Sloane were alone in the living room while the women were freshening up. He and Mike had arranged that he would drop his father and Gay back at his house so that Mike could pick up his own car for the antique expedition while Sloane and Eve took off on their own.

"It won't work." Sloane studied his father's complacent expression, too accustomed to his parent's maneuvering not to be suspicious of the ease with which he had detached Gay from her sister.

Mike turned from his contemplation of the view beyond the multipaned windows. "What won't?"

"Separating the two women."

"From where I'm standing, it looks like it worked very well."

Sloane sighed deeply. In some cases his father could do blank incomprehension better than any man he knew. "You aren't trying to push Eve and me together, are you?" he demanded bluntly.

Mike stared at him, a grin growing wider by the second. "You mean you noticed her?"

Sloane frowned at the surprise he could have sworn was genuine. "You really want to go antiquing with Gay?"

"Of course I do, you young fool. Damn good-looking woman, and she knows a thing or two." Mike thrust his hands in his pockets and glared at his son. "I am not in the habit of lying to women, even for you, Sloane Michael."

Sloane grimaced at the name his father had picked up from Sloane's grandmother. "I believe you." He shook his head, laughing at his own paranoia. "It's just that you've been on my neck since Stryker and Slater tied the knot. I jumped before I looked."

Mike relaxed his stance, laughing a little at both of them. "Actually, I would have done just that if I had thought of it," he admitted.

Sloane shook his head. "I wish I had broken more rules when I was a kid. You deserve everything Slater and Stryker ever thought up."

"What unusual names. Who are they?" Gay asked, coming into the room just behind Eve.

Sloane turned at the same time Mike did. "My brothers. I'm one of a set of triplets."

"Identical triplets," Mike clarified proudly.

Both women's eyes widened. "How identical?" Eve asked.

"Unless you know us very well you wouldn't be able to tell us apart."

"I don't know about that. Joy knows Slater without a miss. And Tempest can definitely find Stryker in a blizzard," Mike corrected after a moment of consideration.

"She probably did at some time or other," Sloane pointed out dryly.

Mike chuckled. "As a matter of fact, I believe my problem-solving son did find her in a snowstorm, trapped on a mountain, dangling from one rope. Told me he cursed steadily for the three hours it took him to get her back on firm ground."

"Tempest said he cussed the whole way down the mountain."

Mike nodded. "Probably did. My generation would have paddled that young woman's bottom until she couldn't sit down for a month. Damn near got herself killed that time and she wasn't even twenty then."

Eve exchanged a look with Gay, finding her own curiosity and amusement reflected in Gay's eyes. "Are Tempest and Joy their wives?"

"For their sins, they are," Sloane said. "They are very special women."

"You'll probably meet them before you leave."

Sloane stared at his father. "They will?"

"Did I forget to tell you? They're coming for a visit. Since you couldn't come to celebrate their news, they decided to come to you. That's another reason why I decided to take up residence here for a while. It will be nice to have a family gathering.''

Sloane shook his head. He should have been used to his family's idea of popping in on a moment's notice. Neither Slater nor Stryker could ever light in one place long enough to grow comfortable. He glanced at Eve. "Are you ready?"

Eve concealed a grin at his harassed expression. "Yes."

He urged her toward the door. "Let's get out of here before he thinks of any more things he has forgotten to tell me.''

FOUR

"This is a wonderful place," Eve murmured sincerely as she leaned against the fence and let the warmth of the sun heat her skin. The day had been one of surprises, but Beginning Now was one of the most unexpected. Like the man beside her, it held so many facets that one could study it for a year and not understand everything. The teams racing across the court, jostling for the ball, cursing when it eluded one man to fall into the wrong hands, the day-care center in the sunny front room of the building they had just toured, the meeting room for adults, the notices of free clinic Wednesdays and parent-child breakfast Sundays were only part of the picture. It was the reaction of those within the paint-fresh walls and on the black court that had held her interest. Sloane was respected here, liked, accepted. All called him by his first name, from the smallest little girl with the angel's smile to the boy/man called Crazy who looked as if he had a knife tucked in his

61

shoe and murder in his heart. And because Sloane had brought her to this place, she had been accepted. No one had shown surprise at her deafness. No one had treated her differently. No one had hovered.

"I really like Beginning Now," she said.

Sloane turned from the action, searching her face. The sun had kissed it with pink, giving the ivory skin a glow that seemed to beg for his lips. He ached. There was no other word for what he was feeling. Even now he wasn't certain why this was the first place he had wanted to bring Eve. The project was barely begun and most of the people within its walls tended to view outsiders with suspicion and silence. The building was huge and, to one who didn't know the full scope of his plans, probably intimidating.

Eve had walked in, looked around each room as though she were really interested, and asked questions. She had also touched the child with a runny nose, crying for the mother who would never come back, the teenager eight and a half months pregnant by a man who was old enough to be her father. She had won smiles from both. The suspicion that should have dogged their footsteps had been visible only for the first few minutes of their arrival. Even his street-gang team had shown a remarkable inclination to accept Eve, inviting her to watch them play.

"I'm glad," he said simply, his fists balling in his pockets to keep him from touching her.

"Hey, man, you aren't watching!"

The sudden shout and the laughter that followed broke the mood. Sloane and Eve returned their attention to the last stages of the game.

Eve laughed softly as one boy, shorter than the rest, suddenly zipped between players and stole the ball. The yells of outrage from his supposed friends only made him laugh as he lunged down court. "I hope they don't kill him," she said, her eyes on the play. The boy rose impossibly high in the air, and at the last second aimed the ball at the rim. It hung on the metal. She held her breath, rooting for his team as she had rooted for the other earlier. Without realizing it, she caught Sloane's arm. "Go in," she commanded, her shout easily carrying across the field.

Sloane tried not to like the feel of her hands on his arm. He tried not to listen to the sound of her voice, its ring of enthusiasm and endearing hesitations. He lost both battles. His own hand settled over hers. Her glance flashed to his face, her smile demanding an answering response. In that instant neither noticed the ball, deciding to obey Eve's order. It scored the winning point. "How do you do it?" Sloane asked quietly, his free hand coming up to tuck a stray tendril of hair behind her ear. He had been wanting to do that all morning. His fingers lingered, liking the heat of her soft skin too much to withdraw.

"Do what?"

Her scent was a light mix that hinted at flowers and spice and summer days. He leaned infinitesimally closer to better hold the fragrance in his senses. "Charm the world."

She studied him, feeling the first crack in the wall she had sensed come up the first time they had met. She didn't understand the distance he seemed intent on fostering. It wasn't hostility, although there was more than a trace of anger in him. She had thought at first it was because of her deafness. But the last hour of watching him at Beginning Now and the way he interacted with those around him had made that conclusion seem doubtful.

"Do I do that?"

He inclined his head, his eyes never straying back to the last minutes of play on the court. "Apparently without any effort at all."

"I didn't know." She felt the warmth of his body touch hers, caressing with invisible fingers. She tensed, then relaxed with each inch that faded between them.

Sloane looked at her mouth, listening to the words she couldn't hear. He wanted to taste her lips. Here in front of a gang of boys who were just learning that once in a while the world could extend a hand without a kick following, he wanted to hold Eve close. He wanted to share his dream for Beginning Now, a dream that even his own family didn't know completely. He thought of the years he had looked for a woman to share with, talk to, be with, and failed. He thought of the two he had believed would give to him all that he was prepared to offer in return. He had been so wrong. Hurting himself and them. He was no longer trusting enough to reach out without thinking, and yet in this moment he wanted to do just that. His fingers flexed, obeying the impulse of his thoughts.

A sudden shout from the court rent the impulse in two, shattering it, saving him. He raised his head, stepping back even as he released her warmth. He saw the disappointment in her eyes and the sudden quiver of hurt that lay in the edges of her smile. He saw, too, the strengthening that went into her backbone at the rejection. That contrast of steel and velvet was as unnerving as everything else about Eve Noble.

"The game is over."

Eve inhaled the heat of the day and the loss of the man. She looked past him to the building that he seemed to care about so much. "I would like to see the children one more time before we go. Would you mind?" she asked, angling her head enough so that she could read his lips without looking him full in the face.

"We've been here for almost two hours. Are you sure you want to?"

"Yes. I like children." She glanced from him to the two teams bearing down on them, wide grins on multi-cultural faces. "Big ones, little ones, rough ones, soft ones. The hope for tomorrow. A picture of yesterday and today. One day I'll have a hope or two of my own."

Sloane closed his eyes against the certainty and yearning in her gentle voice. He felt the pain of her words all the way to his bones and beyond. He thrust his hands in his pockets, fighting the pain and remembering the moment. It was all anyone had and all he would allow to have sway over his thoughts. He reached for Eve, more reluctant than ever to pull her close, but the gang was almost on them and their less-than-careful jostling could hurt her unintentionally.

"Hey, man, did you see us? We slaughtered them," Bonzo crowed, the basketball tucked under one skinny arm. "Am I good, or what?" he demanded of Eve without waiting for an answer from Sloane.

"I'd say you were very good, but I value my skin," she shot back with a grin that caught the group flat-footed. Ten mouths gaped at the words, then laughter came in a flash of crooked teeth and jokes.

Bonzo looked quickly at Crazy, getting a faint nod of approval. "You can come see the pool table and stuff if you want," he offered.

Eve glanced from his face to the ring of expressions looming over and around her. She could almost hear the collective breath they held. Sloane had warned her the last room at the end of the hall was off limits to outsiders and a large number of the staff. It was their place, invitations for the grown-ups they had learned to distrust few and far between. "I'm honored," she said softly after a moment. "I'd really like to see it."

"Got Cokes there, too," Bonzo added, urging her toward the back door.

The group parted around her, then closed beside and behind her, a shield, a rear action guard. The language of the streets was graphic even in the most innocent of moments. These men/children had been taught to survive in a war zone with no name. Durham was better than most, but the rules were the same, the risks as great, and the rewards only one more day of living in a world that offered precious little.

Sloane made no attempt to interfere. The invitation had been a surprise. But the last one, he promised himself silently. Eve had come and conquered with a soft word and a gentle touch. He didn't know how she had done it. She hadn't used her deafness, although she had made it clear from the beginning that she couldn't hear and that those around her would have to make sure she looked at them so that she could answer. The knowledge had had a strange effect on everyone. Beginning Now was a place of meeting but very little physical touching. Eve's disability made that flaw show in all its forms. The hesitancy of others to touch her to draw her attention had lasted for only a few moments of the initial meeting with each person. Then hands came out, small hands, work-roughened hands, clever hands that probably had stolen, and disfigured hands—all had touched her lightly, drawing back the instant the contact was made. It had been enough. Her smile had flashed, strong and sure. Her head had turned, welcoming the touch, curious to answer whatever was waiting to be asked. That kind of acceptance was alien here. That kind of open emotional response so much more than those who came to Beginning Now had probably ever known in their lives. Sloane had stood on the fringes, seeing in this one morning the effect Eve could have on the hurting, the wary, the guarded. She cared so much. Her book had been no more or less than the sum of her truth. Her story had not been sold for the money it could bring its owner but for the hope it could give to others. Her passion was a clear river of feeling that invited all to share in its rare purity. He, as those in this place, ached for that touch, that smile that said nothing was more important than the next moment he would share with her.

Sloane leaned against the door, watching as the children crowded around Eve much the same way as the older ones had done when they had attempted to teach her to play pool. Dark fingers plucked at her blouse, gap-toothed grins matched the barrage of childish confidences that even the last fifteen minutes of concentrated attention had yet to diminish.

"She's wonderful with children," Rita said as she stood beside Sloane and observed her charges enjoying their visitor with the funny voice. "She'd make a wonderful mother."

Sloane's face didn't change with the comment. "She's just as good with the gang."

Rita shook her head, silently envying Eve's ease with others. "She's so natural. She makes you feel good just to look at her."

Sloane studied Eve as she bent down to speak to one little girl who had yet to join the other children. "Kitty still hasn't come out of her shell, has she?" Sloane commented to the teacher, studying the child who had everyone in this unit of Beginning Now concerned with her continued silence. "I was hoping by now we'd see some kind of progress."

Rita frowned at the way the preschooler shrugged away from Eve's touch. "The doctor phoned to discuss the results of the tests he had taken on her. They confirmed what he already suspected. She's completely deaf." She glanced at Sloane. "I've left a message with our silent benefactor about the problem, but he hasn't gotten back to me yet."

Sloane pushed away from the door. "He will. Didn't he promise to make the resources for the situation available if they were needed?"

"Yes. But the thing is, that dealing with a voice on the end of a phone is a lot different from handling a face-to-face. You're the only one who seems to know him and you aren't talking."

Amusement flickered in Sloane's eyes at her disgruntled tone. "I don't want to risk our work."

"You'd think he'd like to see what we're doing. How could a man set up a project like this, solicit donations, keep an eye on us so that every move we make is known to him before we even tell him and still not ever make a personal appearance down here?"

"How do you know he hasn't?"

Rita perked up at that. "You mean he's been here? Don't tell me he's one of your gorgeous brothers."

"I'm not telling you anything." His grin took the sting out of the denial. "But I *am* taking Eve out of here before she faints from hunger. She wanted to come here before lunch."

Rita looked horrified. "You mean you haven't fed the poor woman?"

"It's almost one o'clock." She stepped to the center of the room and clapped her hands twice. The children came to her side, some more quickly than others. "Everyone, let's thank Eve for visiting with us today." A chorus of words followed the command.

Sloane waited while Eve made one last attempt, although unsuccessful, to communicate with Kitty and then led Eve away amid demands for Eve to return. Sloane glanced at Eve's face the moment the door to Beginning Now closed behind them. In the sunlight he could see the fatigue that hadn't been immediately apparent inside. Anger at her own disregard for health surprised them both.

"I should be shot for letting you stay this long without a thing to eat," he announced, taking her arm and linking it with his.

Eve read the words, surprised that her normal irritation at the way others around her seemed determined to shelter her wasn't present. Maybe it was the way he made it plain that he didn't intend to hover, to cosset her to the point of madness. "I hope you don't mind if I eat more than is polite," she replied, feeling pleasantly tired. She slipped into the car seat with a sigh.

Sloane went around to his side and got in. He glanced at her, seeing her eyes close as she leaned her head back against the rest. Answering her would do no good but he did anyway. "The way I feel right now you couldn't do anything I would mind."

Eve looked up as her sister strolled into the living room, looking more tousled and far happier than Eve could remember seeing her. "Did you have a good day?"

Gay dropped onto the couch, kicked off her shoes, and leaned her head back on the cushions. "I had a wonderful day. My feet hurt. I've walked miles. Torn a hole in my new slacks and broken two fingernails."

Eve eyed her sibling's grin and tried not to laugh

at the satisfaction clearly visible in her eyes. "Most people would call that less than wonderful."

"Antiquing isn't any fun if you don't get tired, hungry, and dirty. Who wants to hunt for treasure like you shop for a good dress? No fun at all."

"Did you buy anything?"

"A few goodies."

"How few?"

Gay shook her head. "I'm not saying a word. You'll see when we get home."

"You're having them shipped," Eve guessed.

Gay nodded. "Mike suggested it."

"You like him."

"What's not to like?" She shrugged, then laughed. "He's good-looking and fun to be with. He likes the things I do. He makes me laugh." She pushed off the couch and bent to pick up her shoes. "I'm going to get ready for dinner. Mike knows this really great place for ribs, so we won't be going with you and Sloane like we originally planned." As she headed for the bedroom, she added, "I can't remember the last time I had ribs, now that I think about it."

Eve watched her sister leave the room. She should have corrected Gay's assumption that she and Sloane were holding to their plan to have dinner out. But she knew what would happen. Gay would cancel her dinner, stay home, and worry about the almost-nonexistent shadows under Eve's eyes. Eve didn't want that. She much preferred seeing Gay leave with that smile lighting her eyes, the spring in her step, and the eagerness of her expression. Eve tucked her legs more securely under her and smiled faintly. Mike was a nice man who would take good care of her sister. He'd show her a good time without the kind of man-woman pressure that would surely send Gay into hiding. In short, his age, his manner of treating Gay as someone special, made him safe. She was definitely glad she had decided to make this trip.

Sloane stared at the clock, angry at his inability to concentrate. With Gay out for the evening with Mike, Eve was all alone in the guest house. He paced, glared out the window, and muttered under his breath. It was his responsibility to take care of her. He couldn't leave her there with no way to hear even something as simple as the phone. Mark had only been able to get the doorbell and light arrangement ready in time for her arrival. But the phone was another matter entirely. One box for incoming calls was only as good as the other end of the line having the same setup.

Finally, unable to stay away, Sloane pulled on a light jacket and left the house. The guest accommodations were only three blocks away. He could have walked but decided he might need the car. Eve answered the door on the third ring.

"Is something wrong?" she asked, stepping back for him to enter. She tugged the robe she had pulled on closer, the nip of the evening air more chilling because of the bath she had just finished.

"You're here alone."

She studied his expression and sighed. If he had come because he wanted to, she would have been glad to see him. But to come out of responsibility was something that hurt in a way she wasn't ready to define. "It isn't the first time, and I am over twenty-one."

"You can't even use the phone if you had a problem."

"Actually, I could. Hearing isn't required to convey information. I would dial 911 and explain my deafness and the problem. Or call you."

He jammed his hands in his pockets, keeping his eyes on her face. She looked entirely too appealing in that short pink robe that was modest even by a nun's standards. Her scent was shower fresh, her skin soft in the subdued lighting. He ached to touch her. "You would have no way of knowing if anyone answered."

"Haven't you ever heard of trust?" Eve walked past him into the living room and sat down on one end of the couch, tucking her feet under her. If she was going to get a lecture on the facts of life she lived with daily, she'd at least be comfortable for the reprimand. "I refuse to live my days worrying about what-ifs. It's too confining. I'm deaf. So what. I take normal precautions, but I'll be damned if I'll live in a cotton batting world. I accept it from my family." Anger peeped out of her words, denial of the truth that others would thrust on her. "I won't accept being less than whole with a stranger. If you can't accept that, then that's your problem."

Sloane stared at her, for the first time hearing rather than just seeing the steel he had known existed. "I'm not asking you to be anything."

"Aren't you? You don't want to be here, but I'm your responsibility and you take those very seriously indeed. On top of that I'm deaf." She came close to spitting out the last part of the sentence. She watched his face change, saw his anger rise to meet her own. She was glad. "I won't apologize for what I am. If you are going to treat me like a burden, I'd rather you ask Mark to release you. Give me a map and a rental car instead. Deaf or not, I'm not deficient in caring for myself." She folded her arms across her chest, unknowingly creating a centerfold image that was as tantalizing as any carefully staged pinup.

Appalled at her conclusion, Sloane took a step closer. "I have never thought of you as deficient. You make that impossible." In his effort to convince her that he saw her only as a whole woman, Sloane forgot the things he wanted to keep hidden. "Your strength and courage are in your writing. I didn't think you'd live up to what I found in your book. I hoped you wouldn't." Once started, honesty was addictive and too easy. "But you did." Pulling his hands out of his pockets, he came down beside her. "I want you. Your deafness doesn't have a damn thing to do with that except indirectly. Because of it, what it has changed in your life, you are the woman I see now."

"I don't believe you," she said flatly, challenging him as she had never done any other man. "A man who wants a woman isn't usually angry about it. One minute he doesn't smile, then the next minute he builds an invisible wall with posted signs. He doesn't share an important piece of his life and then regret that he did, as I think you did this afternoon."

"This one does."

Eve studied his face, finding what she had yet to

see. An open path to his thoughts, his emotions. He wasn't a man for calm in spite of the easy way he had with others. There were storms in his eyes, turmoil that carried the scent of danger, of risk taken with no more protection than the blind trust in one's own strength. She touched his arm, feeling the cords of muscles flex, silently rejecting her warmth. Hours before she would have withdrawn, out of respect for another's privacy but also out of her own need to shield herself. She felt neither need now.

"Tell me why you don't want to want me. If I'm going to face your anger, you owe me that at least."

Sloane looked down at her slim hand against the black of his jacket. He had started this. He could evade and end up hurting them both. He could give her stark words to drive her away and deny himself these few days that fate had decreed could be his. Or he could give her a part of the truth. He raised his head. Those eyes. Lying to those eyes that saw more than most of the world even knew existed was impossible. Taking from this woman was equally impossible. She had given up enough of herself to last a hundred lifetimes. "Writers betray so much of themselves when they put word to paper. Emotions, needs, dreams, fears. It lays out like a giant map for anyone caring enough to look. Your book told a very powerful story with simplicity, passion, and compassion. But more than that, you drew a picture of yourself. A woman. A caring woman who loves life. Who wants children. Who believes in the future, the present, and the past. Who sees more in events than just happenings in space and time. You aren't someone for a light relationship. You are the kind of woman a man with eternity on his mind looks for all his life and rarely finds.''

Eve read his lips, finding each word more compelling than the last. No one had ever said anything so moving to her before. No one had ever seen so much. He had painted her far better than she was, but the essential facts of her belief systems and her hopes for her own future were so accurate that he could have walked into her mind and traced the line of each of her dearest wishes. ''And?'' she whispered when he didn't continue.

''And I wanted that a long time ago. But that isn't my fate. It can't be. And I want you. And I think you want me at least a little bit.'' He reached out to cup her cheek. The simple caress was all the more evocative for its restraint.

''You're making a long leap in your thinking.'' Even as her words sought to evade, her body signaled its honesty with a faint shiver of need.

Both felt the change. He with pain and a strange satisfaction. She with surprise and a sense of feminine power that had yet to test its strength.

''That's the way I am. I can't take a moment without seeing the effects it will have on the future.'' Her skin was warming his, her fragrance speaking silent invitations that he fought even as he tried to make her understand.

Eve touched the hand that connected them. ''So what do you want me to do? Deny I find you attractive, interesting, in spite of your moods?''

''It would help.''

''I don't lie.''

''Make an exception.''

She laughed softly, his desperation so quick that, for a moment, she didn't realize how very serious he was. Her smile died, killed by the blaze of passion in his eyes. "You mean it," she murmured, shaken.

"More than I intend to tell you. Tell me you don't want me even a little. Tell me I could be a robot for all you care." His other hand encircled the slender column of her throat. He could feel her pulse accelerate, her life force heating with his nearness.

"I can't." She leaned into his touch. "I want to know you. You're as much a surprise to me as I seem to be to you. I want to take the risk of exploring what I feel."

He cursed shortly, for once hating the truth as he had always hated lies. "I'll only hurt you. Hell, I'll hurt myself just as much."

"Tell me why."

He looked away from her, then back, never closer to betraying his secret. "I can't."

She touched his lips. "You mean you won't."

"Same thing."

"You know better." She traced the outline of his mouth. "It doesn't matter anyway. I want this. Hurt in the future or not, I won't walk away just because I might get my fingers singed."

"You're either braver than I am or more foolish."

Her smile was gentle then, a reflection of what her life had taught her. "No. I still trust in light after darkness, good after bad. You don't. Whatever has hurt you burned that out of you."

"Pity." He tensed against the possibility.

"Compassion. Regret." She leaned close enough to kiss his cheek lightly. "I don't believe in pity.

That drains the giver and recipient. If you want pity, you'll have to go to someone else." She drew back, turned her lips into his palm, and duplicated the caress she had given him. Then she took his hand from her skin, accepting the cold that came with the removal of his heat. "Do you like pizza?"

Sloane stared at her, then the hand she had placed in his lap. He could feel her kisses like brands. He looked up. "Yes. Why?"

"I'm starving. I was hoping you would offer to order out for me."

He blinked, startled at the abrupt switch of subject. For a moment he studied her, then realized there was nothing more to be said for now. She had left the ball squarely in his court. Now she was waiting for the next volley. He almost smiled. The flicker of understanding in her eyes did make his lips twitch. "Has anyone ever called you maddening?"

She shook her head, her expression carefully solemn. "No. My only nickname is Saint Eve."

He laughed then, deeply, unrestrainedly. He took her hand and tumbled her into his lap and pressed a kiss as chaste as the two she had given him on her startled lips. "You may look like a saint and even act like one most of the time, but I have a feeling there is a dare-anything spirit lurking in that seemingly angelic personality."

She batted her lashes at him, happy that she had given him laughter to combat the bleakness that had turned his eyes to barren wastelands of emotion. "If you don't tell anyone, I won't."

He tipped her back on the couch and got to his

feet. "Behave, woman, or the last thing you'll get is a pizza."

"With everything," she shot back.

He nodded, suddenly very glad he had come to her. "With everything."

_____ FIVE _____

"How do you do it?"

Eve licked the last of the pizza sauce from her fingers and sat back with a sigh. The single piece still residing on the large-size circle of cardboard drew a regretful glance. "Do what?"

"Eat like a truck driver."

"I didn't know I did."

Sloane propped his elbows on the kitchen table and eyed her slim form. The much-washed jeans and pullover top she had exchanged for the robe were just as concealing and just as appealing. "Trust me. I know."

She wrinkled her nose at him, her eyes dancing with amusement. "I still can't believe you and your brothers spent your summers in the cab of an eighteen wheeler. In fact, I can't imagine three of you running around anyway." She copied his position. "How does it feel to have two clones of yourself?"

"It depends on the day and circumstances. If I wanted to fool someone into thinking I was in one place when I wanted to be somewhere else it would be very convenient. If I wanted to find my own girlfriend in school it would be damn annoying. Slater always had the girls chasing after him and Stryker was always saving some cute little blonde from the follies of her own stupidity. I fell somewhere in the middle. My girlfriends were the brainy ones, the rule followers. Stryker and Slater occasionally exchanged places on their dates, just to see if they could. I never wanted to."

"Rule follower?"

"No. It just didn't seem fair. I couldn't even make myself play hookey if I could have gotten either one of them to take my classes."

"So your brothers were the devils and you were the angel."

He grimaced at the description. "Boring, more likely."

She laughed, shaking her head. "I don't think you have a boring bone in your body. Certainly those kids down at Beginning Now don't think so."

"They're a special case."

"How did you end up getting involved in that project? Rita said there is a silent backer that only you know."

He leaned back, smiling faintly at her unconcealed curiosity. "And you want me to tell you who."

"Well, now that you mention it." She eyed him hopefully.

He shook his head. "No one knows."

"But you."

He nodded.

"Okay, tell me why the mystery."

"He doesn't like publicity."

"Most people do."

"He isn't most people."

"Does he live here?"

"Maybe."

She sighed. "You could give a clam lessons in silence."

"And you make the curious cat look like a piker."

"Even." She held out her hand across the remains of the meal they had shared.

He took it, tugged on it just enough to bring her out of her chair, and bent slightly across the table. He raised up and kissed her lightly, teasing them both for one second before he drew back. "I've been wanting to do that since you took the first bite."

"You're confusing me with the wrong Eve."

He eased around the table and pulled her into his arms. "And a pizza isn't an apple." He saluted her lips once more, again teasing rather than satisfying. "And I'm not Adam. But you are one tempting piece of female." Another kiss teased her ear. Another her neck.

Eve shivered in his arms, delightful quivers of sensations tracing her skin. Angling her head, she offered him more territory to explore. "You're not bad yourself even if you aren't Adam."

Sloane raised his head to look at her. She had left him with a decision to make. He had made it as he had sat across the table from her and felt the pull of her curiosity, her interest in everything about him. Her smile, the glow in her eyes, were addictive. He could understand now, how those at Beginning Now had succumbed to its allure. Desire had so many degrees. A man could make light love and emerge with no scars. He wanted his emotions to be that easy with Eve. They weren't. They were volatile, invitations to forget the reasons she wasn't a woman to be taken lightly. But if she knew and understood the rules, perhaps, it would be possible to allow their worlds to merge for just a little while. A small taste of heaven would have a high price but it would be worth it.

"We can play a little. I want that and a lot more, but I won't go that far," he said roughly, honesty an acid in his mouth.

Eve read every word, felt the passion held under tight wraps in the way his hands molded her body. She didn't understand his reasons for his decision, but she could not doubt his complete commitment to his choice. "If you are asking if I can play by that rule, I don't know," she replied honestly. "I don't have a lot of experience to draw on."

Sloane had thought that the case and hoped he was wrong. Controlling himself was hard enough. Watching for her needs as well was a fool's errand. But walking away completely appeared equally impossible. He touched her lips, feeling her breath curl around his fingers as though to deepen the contact. Every gesture, conscious or unconscious, spoke silently of her awareness of him. He felt his own body respond unmistakably. "If I had an ounce of self-preservation, I'd talk Mark into finding you another guide." His mouth took the place of his fingers, tracing the fullness of her lips and feeding on her taste. He was breathing hard when he raised his head again.

"Tell me you don't want to play it safe," Eve commanded huskily, her hands thrust deeply into his dark hair.

"I don't."

"Good." This time she was the one to take the initiative. His mouth carried the traces of Italian spice and male. Both demanded appreciation for the subtle differences of flavor. Eve felt the effort he was making in the way he held her without drawing her as near as she wished to be. His warmth was hot enough to heat her skin. She moaned softly, pushing closer.

Sloane forced himself to let her have his mouth and not take more in return. His only chance of staying within the bounds he had set was to permit her to make the pace. But it was hard. She felt so good, her soft body molded to his. His arms tightened for a fraction of a second before he tore his lips from hers. Tucking her head against his chest, he leaned his forehead on the crown of her hair. Neither spoke. Both breathed deeply, each fighting for control.

Eve stroked his chest through his shirt, soothing him, feeling both guilty for what she had done and pleased that she had the power to take them to the edge of the point of no return. He was fire when she hadn't known a flame with this intensity could exist for her. He was wanting until need became pain that hurt to the point of pleasure. He was questions with no answers shared. He was denial with only a promise of a little satisfaction on the fringe of completion. He was the challenge, greater than any she had ever faced. Sloane had named the game and the rules. Fate had decreed the field of play. But neither fate nor Sloane had accounted for her own strategies, her own razzle-dazzle that had taken her out of a world with no sound into the realm of a future with limits set only by her own hand. She had been tested. Gay called her Saint Eve. Her family and strangers saluted her courage. None of them seemed to realize it wasn't courage that drove her. It was an inability to take no for an answer. That was her flaw. She didn't quit. Denial was simply a change of direction or a rock to stand on to reach what she wanted. If she decided that Sloane was the man for her forever, she would not back down, even from him. She would demand her answers, either openly or subtly, but she would prevail. She would fight his demons with or without his help. She would give of herself until he had no choice but to see what they could have together. But she would not quit. She lifted her head from its resting place against his heart.

"I will respect your rules . . . up to a point," she said quietly but with an underlying intensity that only Sloane could hear. "But know this. I don't lose. If you become more important to me than this play that you will allow, I will do what is in my nature to do. I will fight you to hell and back for a future."

Sloane read the soul-deep truth in her eyes with a sense of shock and strange admiration. So that was the fount from which the steel he had sensed had come. The McGuire blood rose to the challenge. Elemental. Primitive. Both called to the deepest sense of his own strength. Woman to man. Unequal in many ways and well matched in so many more. "You think you could win?"

She smiled at that, showing him something no one had ever seen. The steel unsheathed. The naked blade of belief in self and tomorrow. "I have never lost," she stated with beautiful simplicity.

"Neither have I."

Eve felt the fire that she had spent years learning how to direct begin to blaze. "Do you still want to play a little?"

His smile was a tiger's grin of the hunt. He forgot all the reasons why and remembered only the feel of her in his arms and the way she looked right now as she defied him to do his worst or his best. "More than ever."

She stroked his face, her fingernails lightly scoring across the barest stubble of his late night beard. "Where will we go tomorrow? Back to Beginning Now?"

Another challenge. Sloane's grin widened with appreciation. "So you figured out that I was using it to hold you at arm's length." He stroked her cheek, a gentler version of her own caress. "I really did want you to see it."

"Two reasons. But the first wasn't very subtle," she reproved him.

"It would have been for someone who wasn't as adept at seeing beneath the surface."

Her eyes laughed at him as she accepted the compliment. "Your point."

"You have the faculty party tomorrow night," he reminded her.

"Are you trying to tell me I should rest up for the event?"

"Never show an opponent a weakness."

"Good strategy."

He stared at her for a minute, his grin dancing with the devil in his eyes. "How about a tour of the campus?"

"Good move. Definitely safe ground."

He tried to frown at her and ended up chuckling instead. "If this is inexperience, I'm glad I'm not dealing with you when you have experience."

"I said *little*, not *no*."

"Your point." He kissed her forehead before he put her away from him. "Now, behave and walk me to the door. I want to retreat with my honor still intact." He tucked her hand in the crook of his arm. Playing with the flame of his own destruction had never been so intriguing, beguiling.

"I like that word *retreat*."

"Just don't get too used to it." He paused at the door and turned her to face him. "All playing aside, be careful. And be sure that you don't wish for something that will hurt you."

"Now you're the one doing the warning."

"Like you, I play fair." He paused a beat, then added, "To a point."

"It would help if I understood why."

He looked beyond her for a moment, remembering what his secret had cost him in the past. His judg-

ment of women had brought him nothing but pain
and rejection. He didn't trust his senses any longer.
His instincts told him he could trust Eve. Hell, he
wanted to trust her, he thought with uncharacteristic
vehemence. But the risk was great even now at this
early juncture. And later? He didn't want to think
that far ahead.

Eve saw the bleak despair in his eyes and wished
she had not laid a word on the raw wound that lived
in his mind. She touched his face, bringing his gaze
back to her. "I hurt you. I'm sorry."

"I hurt myself," he corrected, giving her that
much. "Not once but twice. Gun shy."

"We all have our bogey men."

He searched her eyes. "I don't see yours."

She couldn't heal his pain, but she could share her
own fear. "I worry that one day I'll love a man and
he'll want me enough to share my body but not the
differences of our worlds. Most people look past
those of us who are different. And I don't mean
just visually look past. We're seen as incapable of
parenting, of holding jobs, of having complete rela-
tionships. They tell themselves they're accepting us,
but they don't even see that one phrase shows just
the opposite. 'Normal, average' people don't need to
be accepted. It isn't a thought process that even oc-
curs. But I, and others like me, have to wait for it."
She shook her head, feeling the surge of anger that
all these years had done little to blunt. She could
control it, but she couldn't eradicate it. "You don't
look through. You didn't even from the first. The
only concession you seem to make for my deafness
is making certain you are looking at me when you

speak. You touch me as though I were any other woman. You don't hesitate, or, at least, not as though my disability . . .''

His hand covered her mouth. Suddenly his anger at the label was stronger than hers had been earlier. "Don't you ever call it that in my presence again," he commanded furiously. "There are two words I damn well won't accept between us. *Handicapped* is the other. You can keep *different* if you like, but the rest doesn't exist. You've killed them if they were ever there."

Tears filled Eve's eyes, shocking them both. "You mean that," she whispered, an old myth that would not die struck down by Sloane's fury.

He caught her close, pressing her head against his shirt to absorb her tears as he wished he could absorb all the blows she had taken for something that had never been her fault. He laid his head against her hair and let her cry, thinking of the tears he had dammed inside that weren't so easily touched. The woman who could not hear who believed in a future with a man and children. And the man who could see no more than today for no future lived in his body for another generation. Fate had a terrible sense of humor.

Josh watched his wife stroll across the bedroom dressed in a couple of veils of nude lace that did nothing to hide her considerable attributes. He knew his Pippa. And he definitely recognized weapons and Mata Hari spy strategy of the Pippa kind when he saw it. His spouse was about to go out of her odd-ball, matchmaking, Machiavellian mind trying to un-

earth his plot to get Sloane McGuire to the altar. He
bit back a grin when a certain very adroit wiggle
managed to unveil a pretty piece of thigh and a nice
set of legs that had a way of holding a man still
when all he wanted to do was buck like an unbroken
stallion.

"Darling." The purr was wicked, male fantasy
and verbal dynamite.

"Yes, dear?" Josh had learned about stealing
fuses early in his marriage. And he hadn't needed a
male fantasy since he had taken this woman to his
bed.

Pippa came down on the bed beside him, laying
her body out in a sprawl that couldn't have been
duplicated by the most practiced courtesan. She studied her male, judging his mood.

He met her eyes, waiting.

Finally, the wicked glint in Pippa's eyes turned
rueful. "You aren't going to let me finesse it out of
you, are you?"

Josh chuckled deeply, plucking his indecently clad
wife off the bed and onto his prone body. "You
haven't got a subtle bone in your body with me and
you know it. I'm on to your tricks."

She pouted at him. "Yes, but it took you a few
years to catch up," she pointed out indignantly.

"True," he conceded, glaring. "You made me
crazy. It was the only defense I had."

"Now you're almost as bad as I am."

Josh thought of his plot within a plot. "I might
just be worse."

She looked interested as her fingers danced up his
chest, managing to find every place on his upper

torso that waited for her brand of teasing. "You might be right. I don't remember ever dangling one of my plots under your nose like a glass of water before a thirsty man."

The flash of pleasure in his expression at her description made her laugh. "I'm better than I thought," he murmured complacently, doing a little tantalizing of his own.

Pippa groaned and wiggled closer. "You don't play fair."

One veil drifted to the floor. "I know. You taught me how not to."

"Dumb me."

"Smart you. I have a lot more fun this way." The last lacy curtain fluttered away, leaving behind skin as soft as roses. Thorns and sweet bounty. That was Pippa and Josh loved her in all her moods.

"I'll give you a hint." He nuzzled her ear.

Pippa tried to keep her mind on the conversation, but thinking around Josh when he held her with nothing but their words to separate them was next door to impossible. "Hint?" she murmured vaguely.

"I'm working on two altar trips, not a choice of women for Sloane."

That brought Pippa to solid mental ground in a flash. Her head came up. "Who?"

"You'll have to guess."

She glared, for the first time in her life ignoring the clever fingers drawing sexy patterns on her breasts. "I won't forget this," she threatened.

He didn't retreat from his woman's strength. He liked her fire and loved stoking the flames just to watch them burn. "I hope not."

"Paybacks are hell."

"You can try," he invited, pulling her head down to meet his lips. Her kiss could have peeled paint. He returned the compliment. Their battle would never be here and both had accepted that from the beginning.

SIX

The campus of Duke University was a beautiful blend of old and new. The original buildings were of multicolored stone set on hills connected by stone corridors and stone-paved walks beneath trees that both sheltered and shaded the haven of learning from the intrusions of the outside world. No city noises were heard here. The winding roads surrounding the original campus were dotted with homes turned administration buildings and frat houses and private residences. Satellite campuses surrounded the heart of Duke. The Medical Center was just one of the later additions.

Eve took a seat on the bench under one of the shade trees on the grounds. Squirrels raced overhead, chattering while a pair of birds chased them through the branches. It was a scene that could easily have belonged in the virgin woods.

"There is something about places of learning. They're a bit like churches in so many ways. The

93

older ones tend to be almost reverential in their bearing, sitting lightly on the land, rising from trees and foliage as if they had always been at one with their site. The newer ones are a little brash, a little arrogant with their modern sculptures and sleek lines, Darth Vader glass. Even the students are different, almost taking on the personality of their alma mater.''

Sloane looked around, listening, seeing with Eve's eyes. Her awareness of the world gave new life to things taken for granted. He glanced back at her. ''You should paint.''

She shook her head. ''Can't draw. Gay is the artistic one in the family.''

''I don't know. You paint superb pictures with words. I think that was what impressed me most about your book.''

''You think about that book too much.''

''It was the first time I met you.''

''Maybe I should get you to write a book. I've watched you with your students and with the kids at Beginning Now. You have a touch that a lot of people would envy. An empathy without being so soft that they can't respect you. You know when to be blunt and when to ease off. That takes something special.''

Sloane looked past her. ''If it's special, you're the only one who thinks so,'' he said, thinking of the times he had been accused of living in a rut.

''I wish I could have her neck between my hands,'' Eve said softly, watching the expressions come and go on his face. The underlying bleakness was painful to see.

Startled, Sloane blinked, focusing on her. "Who?"

"The witch that cut you up," she said bluntly.

"I never said that."

"Well, it sure wasn't Mike. And any man who could have you for a son didn't raise two other sons who were brutal enough to have done it. That only leaves some ham-handed woman."

Sloane had thought he could never laugh about his past. Here in the sun, with all the inhabitants of his world watching, he discovered he was wrong. Wrapping an arm around Eve's delicately boned shoulders, he tipped back his head and let the amusement soar free. Every woman he had ever spent time with had been the exact opposite in build and temperament to Eve. The idea of someone her size taking on just one of his ghosts should have been ludicrous. Instead, all he could see in his mind's eye was a picture of tiny Eve banishing one of his midsize Amazons. It was a very satisfying image for a man who didn't believe in retaliating against a woman even when she deserved it.

Eve felt the sound she couldn't hear, letting it seep into her flesh, bringing a feeling of satisfaction that had few equals. She had banished the bleakness with a smile. She wasn't naive enough to believe the exile was permanent, but it was another crack in what appeared to be a wall of long standing.

"I like you, Eve Noble," Sloane said, hugging her before letting her go. He would have preferred a kiss but that was definitely not on the list of acceptable behavior for a professor of this university.

"Enough to buy me a hot dog?"

His brows rose at the menu. "You only had pizza for supper last night."

"I like junk food." She shrugged and got to her feet.

Sloane took her hand before she could move too far away. "The more I'm around you the more I wonder how your sister could call you Saint Eve." He slowed his long stride to match her shorter one.

"I've wondered that myself, but I finally gave up. Gay can be very stubborn about some things."

They reached the car. He opened the door and waited while she got in. Then he leaned down, touched the tip of her nose as he grinned at her startled expression. "And you can't?"

Eve couldn't remember a time when anyone had ever touched her, played with her, and just talked to her as though there was nothing different about her. Whether he knew it or not, Sloane had given her a gift that could not be measured. As she stared into his dark eyes, remembering the memories that stole the light and the laughter that could brighten the darkness, she felt the first stirrings of love. It was a fragile plant. Tiny. Tender. A bud of life to be nurtured in silence.

"You are a very special man, Sloane McGuire. Whatever comes, I'm glad I know you."

Sloane searched her face, hearing the depth that hadn't been there even the night before. This was no game. No trick. No easy compliment. He wanted to draw back. But the wish went no farther than his thoughts. His hand slipped to her throat where her pulse beat steadily and strongly. A diamond in a velvet-wrapped body. Clear, unblemished, hard enough to defy most forces and capable of being shattered by one well-placed physical blow. A thin line between glory and destruction. Eve.

"I will not regret you, either," he said deeply, letting gravity pull his hand from her warmth. "That is one promise I can make and keep."

"Mark really knows how to give a good party," Mike said as he stood beside his son. Both men were watching the host for the evening introducing Eve and her sister around the room. "If he didn't have those doors to the patio open, we'd suffocate from lack of oxygen with all these people around."

Sloane barely noticed the overfilled great room. He had been here too many times to be impressed by the house Mark had restored to its former glory. It wasn't the set of *Gone with the Wind*, but there were marked similarities in structure and grace.

Mike poked his offspring in the ribs. "You keep looking at Eve like that, son, and everyone in the room is going to know what's going through your mind. I thought you had more sense."

That got Sloane's attention. "What are you muttering about?"

"I said, you're making your interest in a certain young woman damnably obvious." Mike spoiled the effect of his comment with a small grin that conveyed his satisfaction at the reaction.

"Forget it, Mike."

"You can't tell me you don't like her."

"I'm not telling you anything. I'm doing my job just like you are doing yours by entertaining Gay." He glanced back across the room to where the crowd was slowly thinning, leaving a small nucleus of people around Eve. Gay separated herself from the group and made her way toward them.

"I don't see how Eve stands this kind of thing," she murmured with a sigh as she took a place on Mike's free side.

"She likes people." Sloane watched Eve's animated face, the graceful lift and sway of her hands as she spoke. She wasn't signing now, simply using so much of her body, the life coursing through it to imbue her words with her own special brand of power. He hardly noticed Mike and Gay drifting away to the buffet table set up in another room.

Eve moved easily in the crowd, despite her diminutive size, touching this group, that one, pausing to smile or listen intently. Her expressions were varied, a rainbow of emotion to anyone studying the whole. Sloane catalogued each change in her, finding more depth with each passing minute. Even the most reclusive of his colleagues seemed to blossom in the glow of her personality. Folding his arms across his chest, he waited and learned. Then her smile came like a beacon in a small break in the crowd. He frowned, something about that curve of her lips saying more than pleasure in the evening. Her eyes held his. Without even thinking about it, he pushed away from the wall against which he had been leaning and made a place for himself in the sea of people. The waves parted, a path clearing to her side. Her hand slipped in his. It was cold, tense. He didn't look at her, rather at the group gathered around her. He, too, knew how to deal well with people. "I'm stealing her away before she decides we only asked her down here to talk her dry."

A few chuckles appreciated the reprimand. The group eased back almost at once.

Sloane guided her through the opening and past all those who would have stopped them. "Do you want to risk the gardens? It's dark as pitch out there and it's not warm."

"In other words not many are going to brave the elements to follow us," she replied softly.

He glanced down at her then. "My thinking exactly. You looked like you needed rescuing." He stepped aside to allow her to leave the room first.

Eve hesitated just outside the doors, realizing that Sloane had spoken no less than the truth. The patio lights provided illumination for the darkened yard, but it only extended so far from the house. Beyond that, the ebony night was complete. "If we stay here, someone will see us."

Sloane tucked her arm in his. "Then we won't stay. I know the grounds. I promise I won't let you risk life and limb." He urged her beyond the light to the darkness.

"It isn't that." Eve tightened her grip on his arm. "I won't be able to see you. Or you me."

Understanding was immediate. In the darkness Eve would truly be deaf. Without light, she could not see to hear. Sloane hesitated, his hand automatically going to the pocket in which he carried a lighter even though he didn't smoke. "No problem. I have a light with me."

She laughed softly, beginning to realize she could depend on this man to find an answer for most of the curves life tended to throw in one's way. "I should have known."

Neither spoke as Sloane guided them through the darkness to the small gazebo that was situated at the southwest corner of the gardens. The night was alive with scent of spring flowers just remembering that the earth was not always a cold, impossible place. The creatures of darkness played their own melody, as ancient as any ritual known to man. Sloane guided Eve up the two steps to the raised deck of the gazebo, seated her on the soft cushions of the couch at one end, and then flicked on his lighter to find the small candle lamp that usually sat on the table in front of the couch. It wasn't there. Frowning, he scanned the rest of the enclosure then swore under his breath when he realized that only the lighter he held stood between Eve and the darkness without sound.

"Looks like this wasn't such a good idea after all." He sat down beside her for moment. "There is usually a lamp out here for just this kind of thing. But I can't find it."

Eve glanced around. "Do we need it? The lighter seems to be doing the job?"

"If you're comfortable this way, I'm fine."

She leaned back in the cushions. "Then let's stay a while."

Sloane bent forward, pulled the table a little closer, and then set the lighter like a lamp at a safe distance from the edge. "Why did you look like you needed rescuing in there?" he asked when he sat back to study her in the flickering glow.

"Because I did, although I didn't consciously try to send you a message. Your Professor Mullens was just getting into telling me how I could improve my quality of life. A dog for the hearing impaired was probably the least unusual on the list. I'm not good at that kind of thing. No one can know what another's world is like unless that person first lives in it. His attitude is one of the few I don't handle well. I didn't want to ruin the party for anyone."

"So you called me to the rescue." Sloane examined the thought and found that he liked it a great deal. Not because she had been thrust into an uncomfortable position but because she had needed him. He couldn't remember a time when any woman had ever needed him for anything.

"Has it occurred to you that we tell each other things we wouldn't admit to anyone else?"

"Yes." He pulled her close and tucked her against his side. "I've tried telling myself that it's only a normal attraction between sexes, but I'm having a damnable time believing it."

Eve let his warmth drive out the chill of the night. "Me, too. What are we going to do about it?"

"Nothing more than we are doing. We've already established that."

"And if I wanted you anyway? If I were willing to give myself to you in spite of all the questions you won't answer? The future you won't even think about?"

Sloane stiffened, pulled her up and around so that

he could read every nuance of expression in the limited light. "You're crazy. You aren't built that way."

She laid her hand on his cheek, feeling his strength and his anger. Neither frightened her. Both drew her. "For you I think I may be."

"You're weaving dreams and I won't let you. Not about me. I damn well don't want the responsibility."

"You won't have it. It's mine. And I take it without reservation."

"Then you're a fool."

Her hand tightened momentarily on his skin. "No. I told you, I don't quit. I don't run from ghosts, either. I don't understand yours and you won't explain them to me, but that doesn't mean I can't feel them. Can't make guesses."

"Guesses won't help you. You don't know anything."

Eve hesitated. The gamble she was taking was greater than any that had gone before and she wasn't, even at this very instant, certain that what she felt would survive the danger. But she also knew herself. She had to try to reach this man. His armor was formidable. He trusted no one completely and yet he seemed to give of himself at every turn. But the core of him, the essential part that she sensed existed, was tightly locked away from hurt. That was the part she wanted to reach, to understand, and, if she could, heal. She acknowledged the reasons why the last was so important to her. She had wanted to be able to put Sloane in the category of all those with whom she had shared the empathy of one who truly had lived in hell and learned of heaven. But Sloane was not a man to tuck into a neat niche. Not only didn't he fit but he actively sought to slide out of the grasp of anyone who attempted to get close.

"I think you've known pain. The kind that eats at your soul, fills you with darkness when you want to see the light. Only it's never there. It's tied up somehow with children. I've seen a bleakness in your eyes that defies time and space to heal."

At the first word, Sloane drew away from the hand on his face. He wanted nothing to link them now. He had been a fool to open the door that he had done everything in his power to make sure was shut. Angry, not wanting to allow her to see that she had reached him, Sloane retaliated. "You're right. You are guessing."

"You've just proved I'm not." Eve touched his arm, feeling the oak-hard muscles beneath her fingers. "Whatever it is, I wish I could make it better. Life isn't meant for just surviving. It is a feast to the heart and soul if we can only let ourselves believe in it."

The compassion and the understanding in Eve's voice shattered what little remained of Sloane's control. He shunned the warmth of Eve's touch, the sound of her words knifing through the protective armor he had spent years creating and the light that had cast a golden aura over them. Reaction and rejection made him cruel. He shut the cap of the lighter, allowing the night to shroud them in its heavy folds. Because of the tiny circle of light that had lived for a few precious moments, the darkness that followed was all the more complete.

Eve inhaled sharply at the move she hadn't expected. Then she shook off the feeling. A soft touch on a raw wound was often rejected. "You can't hide that easily and we both know it. You can shut me or anyone else out but you can't erase the thoughts in your own brain. They follow you, hounding you until running is just too much effort." Eve sat without moving, her head angled toward his still figure. She hadn't planned this confrontation. The opportunity had been there and she had taken the gift with both hands. The stake was tossed onto fate's table. The cards lay before them now. The wager naked with its cost and its possible reward. The choice to stand or fold was his.

Sloane silently cursed his response to her probing. No matter what she had said, he had not the right to steal her ability to communicate. The lighter dug into his palm as his hand clenched around the metal. His fingers moved with aching slowness to the top. The flame came to life with a single click. The night was no longer black.

"That was unfair of me," he said finally, feeling as though he were forcing the words out.

"Yes." She waited.

"I didn't think."

Eve smiled faintly, forgiving him, liking his honesty. "I never thought you did." She reached out hesitantly, ready to withdraw if he resisted her.

Sloane neither moved away nor toward the slim hand extended toward him. Her warmth curled around his arm, radiating up his flesh, unclenching his muscles and his thoughts. "You see too much," he murmured with a deep sigh.

"Yes." She looked beyond him to the cloak of

moonless night. "I hurt you. Unlike you, I knew I would." Her eyes came back to his, pleading as she rarely did. "I could not lie."

Sloane searched her face, the need to be forgiven she made no effort to hide. "Would you think me dishonorable if I wished you could?"

"No. Human." Her fingers tightened, binding him closer.

"I would feel better if I didn't like you."

Eve exhaled softly. The game had not been played to its last card yet. There was still time, still a chance to win. It was enough for now, more, perhaps, than she deserved. "It would have made it easier on both of us if we had never met. But would it have been better?" Her smile both mocked and accepted the oddities that came with every day. "I don't think so. I'm afraid. I've never been able to admit that to another living soul, but I can tell you. I couldn't have asked my own sister to rescue me tonight, but I reached out to you without even thinking about it."

"And I answered." He cupped her cheek, drawing her close. "Will you hate me if I tell you I wish you had not come?"

"I feel the same. I can't hate you or I must hate myself."

He smiled faintly at her honesty before he bent his head to take her lips. His kiss was gentle, different from the ones that had gone before. It spoke of questions that now must be faced. It spoke of fear that he no longer tried to hide. It spoke of comfort and protection. And binding it all was a need of this man for this woman. He raised his head, his eyes dark with secrets that had always shrouded his thoughts from others. "I won't promise what I can't give. But I will rethink what I thought was written in stone."

She searched his face, realizing what he was offering and the cost of his words. "It is enough."

"But I want something from you as well."

"Name it."

Only their lips moved. They could have been carved in marble otherwise. Every muscle strained against the marriage looming before them of the past and the present. Each had his scars. Both were just beginning to comprehend the risks of this time they wanted to share. "If I can't give you the reasons, you will, for once in your life, let it go."

"Quit?" Even the word was difficult to say. Doing it was asking the impossible. "I never have before."

"That's my price."

"A high one."

"No higher than my own."

"How long?"

"Tomorrow. We have the whole day before you speak at the auditorium."

"That soon."

"We have little enough time as it is or too damned much, depending on our answers."

She inclined her head, accepting the assessment. "All right. I agree."

He pulled her close. "I wish I could tell us both we won't regret this."

She leaned into his strength, having the same wish. "Tomorrow will tell the story," she murmured, her lips pressed against his chest where his heart beat so strongly.

"Win or lose. I wonder which I prefer?" Sloane whispered to the night even as he drank of her scent and absorbed the warmth of a delicate body in his arms.

SEVEN

Sloane lay propped against the headboard of his bed, the darkness of midnight shrouding his bedroom. The night was cool with the faint breeze gently stirring the curtains of the open window. He wore nothing. Needed nothing but answers to questions he hadn't asked of himself in years. He fingered the lighter he held, thinking of Eve. He flicked it once and watched the small flame drive out the darkness. Pure light, powerful enough to dispel the ebony gloom, and yet fragile enough to be at risk from the faintest whisper of air currents. He cupped the flame, studying it as he had studied Eve's writing. So much strength. So much delicacy. She asked things of him. *Demanded* really, just by the way she looked at him with those clear, intense eyes. She touched him, the wounds, the scars. She made him think of things he would have preferred remained hidden. She made him want when he had believed he had controlled his thoughts to such a degree that wanting was no longer possible. Like the flame, she was heat and fire, burning away the darkness with her light and warmth. He had no choice. If he was honest, he knew that he had willingly walked into this time and place with this woman. He had seen what she was in her writing, felt her power, her drive to reach beyond herself. He had been caught then. He had fought but he had been trapped by his own ideals, his lost but not forgotten dreams. For a few moments in time, he had shared with her, telling himself it would be enough. He should have known better. Eve was not a woman for half measures. That, too, he had seen in her book.

The truth. It might steal what little time they had left. But more than that, it might bind them together in chains that even he could not break because, in the end, he would not want to be free. And that was the crux of his problem. He gently opened his hands and let the breeze kill the flame. He had done this to them. He had known what she had not. Now he had to make things right. Tomorrow he would face the truth and kill the flame if he could.

The morning dawned bright and clear, the kind of day that made one smile just for being alive. The birds flitted through the trees, squirrels scampering up one trunk and down another. Eve watched the scene, for once her mind not on the beauty of nature spread before her. She was restless, as she hadn't been in years. She had been up before dawn, showered and dressed, but she hadn't left her bedroom. She didn't want to face Gay until she could bring back even a small measure of her peace. Gay knew her too well in some ways and in others not at all. Gay would see the change in her, wonder and probe. Eve didn't lie well. Gay, like all of her family, was protective, sometimes too much so when she thought her upset. She didn't want Gay's interference in this situation between her and Sloane. Equally, she didn't want to hurt her sister by telling her that. So she waited at the window, knowing Gay was going out once again with Mike. Soon, the house would be hers.

Sloane pulled into Eve's driveway. As he got out of the car, she came down the walk. The sun danced around her, lightly touching the pale-lemon blouse and soft blue jeans. Her hair shone with life and energy, but the smile she offered him was almost shy, hesitant.

"I was watching for you," she admitted when he opened the passenger door for her.

"I was afraid I'd be too early." He wrapped his hand around the back of her neck and pulled her gently closer.

Eve raised her lips, sighing as his kiss settled teasingly over hers. The quiver of nerves that had kept her tossing in bed lost its battle. Sloane's caress stole the restlessness and brought warmth and contentment home to stay. When he raised his head, her smile was real and as tender as his own.

Sloane shook his head, seeing what he hadn't seen before. He didn't have the heart to kill this flame. If it burned him alive he would lie there through every excruciating moment and stand the agony for the reward of holding on to the fire to the last second of his existence.

Eve saw the change in his eyes, the acceptance of something dark in the future but also the need of her now. For the first time since she had met this complicated man, she could read what lived behind the mask he showed the world. "You have decided."

"Yes." He urged her into the car. "But not here or now."

"It doesn't matter. I can wait." She settled into the seat and turned to face him as he got in. "I was afraid you wouldn't share with me," she admitted, then laughed a little. "I haven't been afraid in a long time. But I was about that."

He caught her hand and took it to his lips. "I don't want you to be afraid."

"Don't do this to me," she replied, suddenly urgent when she had just begun to feel calm. "My whole family loves me this way. Protection isn't just a shield, it's a chain, too. I want life, in all its guises. I won't let you take that from me."

He nodded, tucked her hand into her lap, and turned on the car. "I learned that from your writing. That's what I've been afraid of all along."

The drive to the site Sloane had in mind was made in a silence that was rippling with emotions, most under wraps. Sloane glanced at Eve, knowing she watched him more than the spring-touched scenery. He didn't need to fill the silence with words and that, too, was a part of the aura that surrounded Eve. She didn't use sound to mask what she felt. He took her hand when they left the car under the shade of the trees. A narrow path led up a hill and beyond it to a small valley.

"This is beautiful," Eve murmured as the forest wrapped around them, welcoming them into its heart. "But it looks like private land."

"It is." Sloane stopped on the rise of a small hill overlooking the narrow slip of clear water that cut diagonally across the property. Pulling out a blanket, he spread it over the ground. Only then did he look around. "I own it."

"And the house in town?"

He nodded as they both sat on the blanket with the picnic basket taking up the third corner. "One of my brothers does a lot of investments. He has something of a golden touch in that area."

"A strange kind of investment for a man who swears he won't marry."

Sloane looked away from her for a moment, seeing the land as a stranger. It was a piece of real estate that cried out for a family home, children, and all the pets they could desire. "I know." He looked back at her. "It needs a house up here. People to enjoy the view and the freedom."

Eve moved closer, feeling waves of pain lap at her even from this distance. Every time Sloane spoke of family, dealt with children, she felt the same despair, the bleak acceptance that she saw in his eyes now. Guessing would have been easy, but the look on his face had always demanded that she not try to find an answer. It had to come from him.

"Tell me," she commanded softly, sliding her hand into his.

Sloane studied the link between them. It was easier

than looking into her eyes. But he had to look for her to hear. He raised his head, remembering too vividly the two other women and their reaction to what he was about to say. The memories still had the power to sting. Eve wasn't those women. She was more. She loved children. He had seen it in her, watched the way they related to her and heard from her own lips her wish for her future.

"I won't marry, because I won't ask another woman to live with me knowing I won't ever be able to give her children," he stated quietly, every trace of emotion erased from his voice. He watched the knowledge sink into her mind. Saw the shock, the compassion, and the empathy of one who had lost something as important in its own way.

"Tell me the rest."

"Isn't that enough?"

"You know it isn't. Adoption. Artificial insemination. There are a number of ways around this."

The twist of his lips at her reply contained no humor. "You're right, you don't quit."

"And I don't run. You haven't given me a reason why this is so damn impossible."

"I read your book."

"You keep saying that as though it explains everything."

"It does." He caught her close. "Haven't you wondered at the way we are drawn to each other, the need that no amount of caution on either side can kill? Damn it, Eve, I read your words. You write from your soul, your heart. Anyone with eyes can see what you are. You're like that stream." He nodded toward the water. "Clear. Pure. Relentless."

"You're the only one who has ever seen that in me."

"Maybe because the others see only with their eyes. I don't know. I just know when Mark gave me that damn book to read, I lost the ability to walk away from what I am. You made me start wishing when I had put away my dreams. I don't want to hope, damn you. It hurts. Men aren't supposed to hurt. But I do." His hands marked her flesh in his need to make her understand. "My brothers rode the roads with my father and loved it. I hated it. I wanted a home, a bed that was in the same place the next day. I wanted friends, not chance-met strangers with a smile. Stryker sees life as a series of problems. He steps back from everyone and everything. Only Tempest reaches past that distance to the man. Slater is the same in many ways. He has seen death and learned to beat the Fates by living for the second and taking no one into an uncertain future with him. Then a woman named Joy walked into his life and showed him what he would become in the end. He saved her and himself. And she saved his life. My brothers found their own salvation. But it cost. Both sides. I could stand that. I would accept that and thank every god there is that I had a chance at a future I had thought lost. But I can't accept asking someone who has lost something so precious to give up another gift of value. Better to stop it before it had a chance to begin. You could call me arrogant and you wouldn't be wrong." He searched her still face, looking for some sign she understood. "I wanted to protect you and myself. I wanted to be with you but not take from you. You have lost enough. I won't risk making it possible, through me, for you to lose more.''

Eve froze, every muscle in her stilling. Not waiting. Not hoping. Not thinking. The stillness was born of rage. Soul-searing, thought-firing anger to the bone of existence. Very slowly, she raised her hands and pulled his from her body. He watched her, waiting. She edged away from him and rose. Each gesture, each stretch and pull of muscle over flesh required concentrated focus. If she said a word, she would regret every syllable.

"Talk to me, Eve."

She walked to the edge of the hill and stared at the water. She didn't hear him join her. But she felt him. Felt his need, his hope, his despair. For the first time in her life, she wanted to strike out, to cause pain such as she knew to another. "I have never hated anyone. I have never wished harm on a soul. I have never screamed in the darkness at the hand that took my hearing. I have lived the best I knew how and asked only that others let me do that." The words were almost gentle in their delivery. "You have no right." The gentleness ran from the rage unbottled and poured into the last four words. "You had no right to make this choice. You had no right to shut down on me because of your own fear." She laid her hand on his chest, connecting them although they had never been farther apart. "I am a thinking woman. I feel. I dream. I hurt and I cry. I do not recognize nor do I accept less of myself because I am deaf. I don't expect or want others to accept less, either. Only my family has ever come close to having that right and then only because they have been hurt by my deafness far more than I. I owe them so much, I have taken their need to protect. But I won't take it from you. You say you know me. You didn't see that. The most important thing about me and you didn't see that. You are the second man in my life to try to take my right to choose under the guise of protecting me. I am not a child in a grown-up body. My deafness doesn't make me mentally deficient.'' The tears shimmered in her eyes. She looked through them, seeing the agony he didn't hide. Now, when she didn't want to know, he showed her all that he felt. ''You didn't give us a chance out of fear. And then you have the guts to lay that at my door.'' Her hand dropped. ''I think I could hate you for that.'' She started to walk away.

The lock on Sloane's thoughts snapped as she turned to leave him. He caught her. She swung on him, fighting his touch as she had never done before. He lifted her in his arms, stealing the leverage her smaller size demanded to equal the battle. ''You can't hate me. You want to, but you won't be able to do it any more than I can walk away from you. You want me. It's a fire in your belly like it is in mine. Be angry. I am, too. Hate what I tried to do for you if you must. And what I tried to do for myself. I was living with a woman who wanted children when I found out I couldn't give them to her. Unlike you, I had no illness, nothing to pin the blame on, only a bunch of tests that took away a right I had always taken for granted. Suddenly, I was less than a man and the woman I thought I loved let me know that in no uncertain terms. She hated the idea of adoption. She didn't want a gene pool mix with who-knew-what for a son or daughter. You know what I felt. Your deafness has given you the ability to understand that kind of rejection and the scars it leaves. I didn't quit then. I tried again. This time with a woman who showed no signs of wanting children. Again I gave her the truth, only this time suddenly I became half a man. She didn't want my seed in her womb, but she didn't want a man who couldn't put it there, either. I was less than whole.'' Bitterness laced with anger and frustration. His eyes burned with it. His words dripped with the concoction and ripped the silence of nature in hundreds of pieces with every sentence.

Eve lay in his arms, caught between earth and sky, held there only by his strength. Unearthly agony lay in his dark eyes. His soul was torn in fragments. His thoughts twisted with a past he couldn't change. Her own rage died. It couldn't live now.

"Damn you, don't pity me!''

She touched his face, cupping both hands around the lean bones. He flinched at her touch, his eyes fighting her attempts to give him solace. "It isn't pity,'' she whispered, her tears welling again, this time for him. She raised her lips to his, brushing over the thin line, trying to warm the coldness she found there.

Sloane held his breath, no longer sure what was right or wrong. "Then what is it?'' he demanded hoarsely.

"An apology.'' She wrapped her arms around his neck, no longer running from him or what he had done. "Sometimes I'm not only deaf, but blind, too.''

His hands gentled, cradling rather than imprisoning. A step took him to the blanket. He went down on his knees and laid her before him. He searched her eyes, looking for the truth. And finding it. "I didn't want to hurt you."

"I know that now."

"I still don't want to hurt you."

"We are past the point where either of us can protect the other from that happening. We can't go back. You know that."

"But we can stop here."

She shook her head, her hair fanning with every movement. "No." She touched the first button on his shirt. "It's too late. I want you. You want me. We have been burned and now we both know where and how."

"You're sure?"

"No." She smiled faintly. "I'm not sure about anything except that I can't walk away from you without trying. You hurt me. More than anyone ever has. You couldn't have done that if you didn't matter. I have to know how much. If a sword is to be a superb weapon of war or defense it must first be tempered in the heart of a fire, pounded by strength greater than its own and then plunged into the icy depths of water. Isn't that the same with being human? Aren't we born in agony of pain, tossed about by circumstances over which we have little control? Do we not learn from our mistakes? You are a teacher. Don't your students learn more from what they don't know than what they do? Do we not value what we fight for more than what we are given?" Her hand came up to touch his face. "You

are not a coward. Neither am I. I will take a chance
with you, but only if you will grant me the same
gift. No time limit. No control. Let us take what lies
between us and follow it. Fires of hell or gates of
heaven. We'll learn from either. Grow with both.
Together or apart, I think it is worth the risk. Do
you?''

Sloane wrapped his free hand around Eve's wrist,
feeling her pulse accelerate with his touch. He had
never turned away from a challenge. It was in the
McGuire blood to play and beat the odds. He wanted
her with every atom of his being.

"I'll take the risk," he said roughly, consigning
the last of his memories to the past and slamming
the door on them. He and Eve would write their own
future. "As you say, the gates of heaven or the fires
of hell.''

Eve reached out then, taking his hands and carrying them to her breasts. She had never offered herself to any man. Her experience had come out of a
man's curiosity of sleeping with the deaf girl. He
had been gentle, but there had been a distance that
had denied her the right and privilege of feeling a
real man's passion and need. He had marked only
her body with his possession. Not her mind nor her
heart. Those she had held safe, innocent, until this
moment and this man.

Sloane looked at her hands on his, the gift she lay
before him, the risk they both shared. The fire was
burning, encircling them. Destruction or rebirth?
They would learn together. His hands cupped her
breasts gently as he watched her eyes. They didn't

waver as the heat wrapped closer. Her scent surrounded him as she lifted her arms to his neck.

"You are more beautiful than anything I have ever seen. More perfect." He stroked her lightly, tracing her shape through her clothes. He had no wish to rush the moment. It was theirs to savor to the last ounce of pleasure.

"I love the way you have with words."

His lips curved as he flicked open the first button on her blouse. Her skin peeked through the opening, glowing pink and velvety in the mottled sunlight filtering through the trees sheltering them. "I have a way with other things, too," he murmured huskily.

His smile became hers. "Do you?" She traced the back of his neck and shoulders, drawing patterns of sensations over the taut lines. "What kind of things?"

His hands swept lightly down her length, outlining her form, the curves, the hollows, the secret places. Her gasp of surprise mingled with the pleasure flashing in her eyes. "That kind of thing." His lips drifted over hers, teasing and then retreating far enough so that she could read his words. "And that."

Eve arched closer, caught by the gentleness, the tantalizing hints of the passion she had never fully known. "More," she commanded throatily.

"It would be better in a bed."

"No, it wouldn't."

He touched her lips with his forefinger, tracing their fullness, aching to kiss her but knowing she wouldn't be able to hear him if he did. So he teased them both as he answered her need to talk. "There may have been a man, but he taught you precious little."

She searched his face. "Do you mind?"

"No. I do mind the responsibility of it. It would have been easier to take you, and I don't mean just physically." He flicked the next two buttons of her blouse open until the soft tops of her breasts and the lace of her bra were visible. He drew a line along the fabric, smiling gently at the way she cuddled closer, her breath catching with each new intimacy. "I want you to remember nothing but joy in my arms. I want to be every fantasy you've ever had."

"Then kiss me and stop talking." She lifted her mouth, aching in so many ways.

"I don't want to rush you." He leaned down, taking her lips as his fingers slipped past the barrier of lace to the warmth beneath.

Her mouth opened in a soundless sigh. He deepened the kiss, exploring her with gentleness and passion that heated the need to a flame that demanded more fuel. Eve held him close, following each caress, learning and returning the heat and passion that came with every new touch. His desire was strong enough to steal her thoughts and leave behind only sensation and fire. Even as he brushed the blouse from her shoulders, she pulled his shirt from his body. His chest covered her breasts, the whorls of dark hair creating a nesting place for her aching nipples. Sloane lay back on the blanket, pulling Eve on top of him. He lifted her higher so that he could kiss the pink buds blossoming for his need. The soft moans that Eve made tightened his body, demanding immediate freedom from the restraint her inexperience imposed. He ignored the pain of desire unfulfilled and concentrated on the woman who had accepted his flaw with an honesty so pure that he didn't care what he couldn't do, only what he could.

Eve drowned in the sensation of possession by his warm mouth. Every muscle was tensing, reaching out for more. The clothes on her lower body were an irritant. "Take them off." She looked down, her eyes brilliant with wanting. "I want to feel all of you."

"Slow down, honey."

Obeying the need to move, her hips thrust against his. "I can't. Stop worrying and let me get close to you. Let me be yours." She pushed against him again, demanding more than his gentleness. She wanted his fire, and to hell with his control.

Sloane might have been able to ignore her words. Or he might have been able to ignore her body. But not both. Eve was all woman, strong, fearless, born to lie with a man without tricks, illusions, or pretty promises. His hands slipped down her sides to the belt to her jeans.

She sat up, her legs on either side of his thighs and unbuckled his belt at the same time. Two zippers whispered freedom.

"Lie down beside me for just a second," Sloane commanded.

Eve slipped off him and onto the blanket. The moment she was prone, he pushed the jeans down her legs, and then her panties. The air was cool on her heated skin, but she didn't flinch from the nip of the breeze or the hungry look in his eyes as he stared at her as no man had ever done. "Do I get to do yours?"

He shook his head as he caught her hands when she would have reached for his jeans. "No. I'll lose it if you do. Next time, all right?"

He rose and stripped in an economy of motion before coming back to her. He lay down and pulled her back on top of him again. "You will be able to control our joining this way." He touched her lips when she would have protested. "Not that kind of control." He nudged at her hips, letting her feel the danger that lay in a man's strength against a woman's softness.

Eve's eyes widened as she began to realize just the kind of gift he was offering. Any protest she might have made died. Her smile was as tender as her touch. She leaned down, tracing his lips with the tip of her tongue. "I want you."

He cupped the back of her neck and deepened the kiss. Words no longer mattered. His hands found more places to pleasure. Her moans came in soft gasps of sound that only he and the elements of nature could hear. At another time he would think of her loss and the way it would always steal precious moments from her. For now, he cared only for the fire that was fast blazing out of control. When she raised on her knees, a smile of acceptance for the joining that was to come glowing on her face, he knew that as long as he lived no picture in the future or past would ever have such power to lift him above himself or throw him beyond the reach of redemption.

Woman, her name was Eve.

With a thrust, Eve became his. The fire swept over them. Need played music for the dance that had begun with the creation of life. Desire wrote the melody for the sounds that whispered to the trees and the sky. And when the peak rose like an unscalable monolith, his strength was there to lift them over the top. Her softness was there to cushion their fall back to reality and the present.

Silence came with the spilling of the seed that would never bear fruit. Even the land held its breath, respecting the moment and the cost. His hand stroked her hair, his eyes traced the still leaves of the trees rimming their clearing. Her breath was a mist of warmth against his neck. He had never felt so complete. For once, he allowed the illusion, basked in it and cherished it as he had cherished the woman who had given him this moment.

"Are you all right?" he asked softly, for the first time since he had met Eve forgetting that she had to see him to hear.

Eve felt the rumble of sound pass through his chest. Touching her fingertips to his lips, Eve didn't raise her head. "Say that again."

Sloane repeated his question slowly.

"Better than I can tell you." She lifted her head then to smile at him. "So much feeling. So beautiful." Her fingers waltzed over his mouth. She hesitated, for the first time in a long while damning her deafness. "What did it sound like?"

"Heaven."

She searched his face, finding nothing but the truth in his eyes. "What does heaven sound like?" she whispered.

"You." He brought her head down until their lips met. His mouth formed the words but not one sound emerged to taint the silence. "Just you."

EIGHT

Sloane stroked Eve's hair, finding the feel of her pressed to his side pleasurable in a way that was new. There was contentment in the silence, completion. He touched her face, lifting her chin so that she could see him talk. "Did I tell you that I can sign?"

She outlined the fingers cupped against her breast. "No. Mark did."

"You don't use it very much."

"I know. Lipreading gives the people around me the illusion of my hearing." It was easy to tell him what she had never admitted to her own family.

He frowned at that, realizing in spite of all the things he knew about Eve, there were still many gaps. "Do you think I need that illusion?"

She shook her head, smiling. "No. With you I do it more out of habit than need." She sat up, turning so that she faced him. "Shall I sign for you?" she asked with her hands.

Sloane followed the graceful, gentle movements of

her gestures. Ever since he had known Eve was coming he had been practicing his skill. He wasn't quick but he could handle the speed with which she was communicating. "Yes."

"What shall we talk about?"

Sloane chose his gestures carefully, hesitating once or twice. Eve caught his fingers, changing the position slightly to make the movement correct. "Why are you doing this?" she asked aloud, her hand still linked with his.

The words came simply, with complete truth. "It's part of you. Like your hair, your eyes. I don't want just pieces. I want it all."

"Because of this?" A sweeping arc marked their nakedness, the seclusion, the desire that had blazed and gentled to a warm glow of closeness attained.

"Partly." He used their link to tumble her across his bare chest. Her breasts settled in the thicket of dark hair, resting there as though they were coming home. "But most of all because I want to be with you every way I can. You're sunshine on a rainy day. Laughter and warmth. Heat to take the cold away. You fill a need that I've lived with and accepted for so long."

Eve absorbed the words, unable to doubt the depth of emotion that drove them. Men, in her limited experience, didn't give of their feelings with the ease that Sloane could show at times. He held nothing back. He spoke of his flaws with honesty. He told of his need unmarred by pretty phrases that could have been a prelude to her seduction. He had given her passion, then he had given her words. He hadn't used one to achieve the other.

"One more tie," she murmured.

"I know."

"Another risk."

"I know that, too."

Her fingers traced his lips and his smile. "I was worried you would regret this."

"I wondered if you would." _

Their eyes held as his hands swept down her back, relearning the places that gave her pleasure.

"Never." Her smile joined his with a kiss. The silence was filled with the sound of loving. The sun kissed their nakedness. The trees sheltered their joining. And the day slowly drifted toward its change into night before the loving was done, the silence reclaimed by the forest and the creatures who called it home.

Eve hummed as she dashed into the shower. She was late. Normally, she would have been irritated at her laxity but not today. The time with Sloane had been more than she could ever have imagined. They had talked of simple things, important things, funny things. He had told her tales of Stryker and Slater, their wives. She had countered with stories of her own family. He had told her of his role in Beginning Now. She had listened to the commitment he had made which he had kept so closely hidden. He gave out of kindness and compassion to those in need. Glory did not figure in his plans. With every word, Eve found more to admire in this multifaceted man. He was gentle and stubborn. Quiet but with a sense of humor that saw what others often missed. He loved his family but he wasn't unaware of their flaws and he valued their virtues. He walked his own road without apology. But more than all of those qualities, he listened to more than she said. For the first time in her life, someone looked at her and didn't see her deafness first. It felt good to be a whole person, to look in a man's eyes and know he cared for the *woman* not the *deaf* woman. She smiled as she dried the moisture from her body. Sloane had teased her with the signing, making her laugh when he had told of his first attempts at the silent communication. Belting on a robe, she walked into the bedroom, still smiling, to find Gay sitting on the bed, completely dressed for the evening ahead.

"That must have been some picnic," Gay murmured with a grin.

"I enjoyed it," she replied, laughing. She sat down in front of the mirror and began making up. "You look as if you had a good day as well." She studied the sun-kissed glow of Gay's skin, the laughter in her sister's usually serious eyes. "You're looking very rested, revitalized."

"Mike's been a good guide," Gay agreed, glancing down to readjust the full skirt of the rose silk dress she had chosen to wear. It was new, different from her usual neutral style and color.

Eve paid only scant attention to the cosmetics she was smoothing on her face. "I like that. I haven't seen it before, have I?"

"No. I just got it today. Mike showed me a really nice mall. We had lunch there."

"Better you than me. I can't think of a worse fate than dragging in and out of stores. They never seem to have what I want." Eve rose and went to the closet. "If you didn't like to hunt for just the right outfit and if you didn't have exquisite taste, I would have to do my own shopping." She shivered theatrically as she pulled out a froth of pale lavender with tracings of silver detail on the fitted bodice. The delicate color suited her and was a favorite for evenings like this.

"I think you just say that so I'll have something to do for you."

Eve shot her a sharp look, disturbed by something in the wording. "Meaning?"

"It's just until this trip I didn't realize how little you need me around." Gay searched Eve's expression. "Why didn't you tell me?"

Eve hesitated. She had spent so many years trying to let her family love her in the only way that seemed to work for them that it had never occurred to her that any of them would notice the way she really was. Now, faced with the reality, she was momentarily at a loss. "There isn't anything to tell."

For once, irritation touched Gay's face, flashing in her eyes as she got to her feet. "Isn't there?"

Eve frowned at Gay's expression, surprised at the touch of anger. "What's wrong?"

"I have a better question. Just how long have you been letting me think I was helping you? Just why did you talk me into setting up a living arrangement with you after Ross? You were doing fine at our parents' house."

Eve went back to the dressing table to put the final touches on her hair, giving herself time to evaluate the unexpected challenge. "I told you at the time."

"Maybe," Gay conceded, watching Eve closely.

"Maybe you did need to make a life for yourself outside our parents' range of protection and love. Maybe it was time for you to be independent, but the timing was definitely suspect. You had said nothing about wanting to move until I came home with my tail between my legs."

Eve studied her sister, the hurt in her eyes beneath the anger. Eve sighed deeply, realizing that it was time for the truth between them. "You'd had a terrible deal. I loved you. I thought we could both be a help to each other. You needed a place to lick your wounds and I needed to make my own way."

Gay inclined her head, the answer no less than she had expected. "I could have lived with that if you had put it that way then."

Eve absorbed the accusation, feeling her own anger stir. "I didn't lie to you."

Gay glared at Eve, too caught up in her own needs to see her sister's. "You didn't tell me the complete truth, either."

"You were hurt. I didn't want to add to that." In spite of the pain she was feeling, she didn't want to fight with Gay. She rose and went to her, laying a hand on Gay's arm. "You are my sister and I love you. I don't regret what I did. Are you trying to tell me that you do?"

Gay looked down at the slender hand that seemed to mock the word *work*. She glanced up, defensive, angry, feeling a stirring of rebellion that frightened her. "No. But I don't like feeling as though I have been riding on your coattails for the last few years. I thought I was giving as much as I was getting."

Even now she couldn't believe how blind she had been.

"You are."

Gay shook her head, unsure what she meant but knowing the feelings coming to life inside her were very real and very disturbing. "No. I think as usual you're being Saint Eve and this time I'm the one on the receiving end of your largess."

Eve drew back as if she had been slapped, her hand falling away. Gay caught the flash of pain undisguised and swore as she never had in her life. "Eve, no. I didn't mean that."

Eve backed away from Gay's touch. She had thought she was immune to the things others could say. She could see the contrition on Gay's face. She felt it, but it didn't take the hurt away. Nothing would. Not apology. Not denials. The words had been spoken out of feelings that existed. "It's late. We have to go." She collected her handbag and left the room.

Gay followed, angry now with herself as she hadn't been before. "Please. I didn't mean it," she tried to explain as she managed to get Eve to look at her.

Eve shook her head, halting the explanation which wouldn't change anything. "No more. I have to be at the auditorium in a few minutes. Sloane should be here by now."

The sound of the car pulling into the drive couldn't have been more poorly timed. "I'm sorry." She spread her hands. "I hurt you, and that was the last thing I meant to do. I don't know what's wrong with me."

Eve sighed, unable to bear seeing Gay's pain. That hurt nearly as much as her own. She had not questioned her way of dealing with her family until this moment. She needed to think, reevaluate. But there wasn't time. Gay's need was now. She touched her arm lightly, smoothing the dark emotions from her thoughts. "I know you didn't mean it. It's hard when things change around us without warning. I understand. Really I do." She tried a smile, praying that it and her words would give her sister ease.

Gay searched her eyes, finding forgiveness that she didn't deserve. Eve had never been anything but good to her. Because Gay knew Eve's moods, few though they were, she realized that the subject was buried as far as her sister was concerned. She would not bring up the hastily spoken words ever again. Gay had never understood Eve's ability to accept the unpalatable and go on. She didn't fight although she was no coward. Rather, she seemed to dig into herself, creating a barrier that was invisible until one tried to reach past it. Gay could feel that barrier now even as Eve gave her a way to retrace her verbal steps to what had been. Frustration mixed with anger. A dangerous combination. Gay wanted to shake her sister, demand that she fight back, talk to her, not remove herself mentally from the problem. But there would be no fight. Not now. Not ever.

"Sloane's here," Gay said finally.

Eve accepted the words with a nod before heading for the front entrance. She would think about what had happened between them later. She would find whatever answers she needed without demanding more of Gay than she could give. She opened the door to Sloane and gave him her best smile.

Sloane took the hand she held out, searching her face, sensing tension that he had never felt in her presence. There was no clue to be found in Eve's expression. He looked beyond her to where Gay stood. Eve's tension was very much alive in her sister.

"Are you ready?" he asked quietly of Eve.

"Very ready." She tucked her hand in the crook of his arm, leaning against his strength. She hadn't realized she needed him in that way. She had spent her life learning how to fend for herself, depend on her own abilities. Drawing from another had seemed wrong, weak, until now.

He glanced at Gay. "Mike had a phone call just as we were leaving. He said he'd come here for you or you could go with Eve and me."

Gay studied her sister's back, then shrugged helplessly. "I'll wait. Eve really doesn't need me."

Sloane frowned at the emotions clouding the words and the way that Eve was ignoring their conversation. Neither woman's reaction was usual. "He shouldn't be more than five minutes. He was talking to my brother Slater."

"I'll wait." Without saying anything more, she closed the door, leaving Sloane and Eve on the porch.

"We're going to be late if we don't hurry," Eve murmured. She had felt the door shut behind her.

"We have time," he replied as they headed down the walk. "Did you and Gay have words?"

"You could say that." She got into the car, settling her skirt around her.

Sloane touched her cheek, drawing her eyes to his. "Let me help. You're upset."

She tried to smile. Tears were close, and that surprised her. "Don't be nice to me right now," she whispered, feeling vulnerable. All she wanted to do was lay her head on his shoulder and cry. Saint Eve. How she hated that name.

Sloane caught the glint of moisture in her eyes and his frown deepened. Whatever had occurred was no small problem. It had cut deep. The Eve he had begun to know didn't cave in over nothing.

Eve wrapped her hand around his wrist. "Please, Sloane. Not now. I have to give that speech. If I talk about it, I don't think I'll be able to get up on that stage." She hesitated. The words in her mind were as new as the myriad of emotions that Sloane had shown her existed. For the first time in her life, she was asking someone she loved for something for herself. "Help me by not probing."

Eve couldn't hear the desperation in her own voice but Sloane could. It hurt. Too much. But he was past the point of being warned by his own reactions. She mattered too much. He turned his hand, catching hers in his warm palm and carrying it to his lips. "All right. But I'm here."

"Thank you," she whispered.

His smile was as gentle and compassionate as hers had been to him on so many occasions. "My pleasure, pretty Eve."

Her smile was a shaky effort but it was a beginning. "Only pretty?"

He touched the corners of the trembling lips. "Make this real and I'll call you beautiful." He outlined the curve of each lip before bending to kiss the smile that was growing stronger by the second. When he raised his head, she was almost her serene self again. The pain lay in her eyes, but unless someone looked closely it would not be seen. "Are you ready?"

"Yes."

"And now, ladies and gentlemen, I give you Eve Noble." The dean turned and extended his hand.

Eve stepped onto the stage, smiling at the audience. The auditorium was filled to standing room only, she realized as she scanned the faces turned toward her. Even after six years of public speaking she still discovered a kind of shock in the number of people who came to see and hear her. Her eyes skimmed over the third row where Gay and Sloane's father sat. She took the dean's hand, allowing him to lead her the rest of the way to the microphone.

She stood for a second, looking out over the sea of faces, feeling the need, the curiosity, absorbing both. "I thank you for the welcome. And no, I can't hear it but I can see your hands clapping and your expressions. There is a world of information in body language and facial changes that I rely on now that my hearing is gone. *Lost*, you would say." She smiled at the silent crowd. "My world is changed. I hear with other parts of my senses." As she spoke, she signed. Then she stilled for a second, holding her hands visible above the podium. "I speak with these . . ." She touched her lips. "And these." Her hands traced a beautiful arc before resuming their silent translation for those of her listeners born or made such as she.

Sloane's eyes followed every graceful movement of Eve's hands, his ear caught every inflection of her softly blurred voice. He listened without moving, part of his concentration discovering that those around him were equally caught by this extraordinary woman. She smiled as she spoke of her deafness and no one, least of all himself, seemed to find that odd. She told of treasures to be found in silence. Of reaching beyond one's self to the strength that lived in every heart and soul. Eve didn't preach. She didn't need to. She was a living example of the best of humankind. Her words lodged deeply into the silence that rippled with every sound flowing from her lips.

Sloane had thought he understood her. Her writing had drawn him from the first. Then her picture. Then the woman herself and the fire that slumbered in her eyes. He had danced with the fire, been burned and reborn in its heart. He had felt his life changed from the first moment of Eve's impact. He knew that whatever lay in the future for them, he would not regret this time with her. She had given him pieces of himself he hadn't realized were missing. She had held up a mirror to himself and the world, forever altering the way he perceived both. But in spite of all that she had given him, he had discovered that there was much he could offer her. The serenity that cloaked Eve in shimmering veils of peace was costly. He had seen what she gave without thought to herself and he had seen the physical, mental, and emotional toll. He had thought her family understood. And they had, up to a point. But listening to Eve's tales of her childhood and later years he realized that while her parents and siblings supported her every endeavor, they didn't seem to recognize the eagle chained in the sparrow's body. Eve was determined to soar in the heavens. She wasn't just content to fly. Her family seemed to see that as some sort of compensation syndrome. He didn't think so. Eve would have soared no matter what her body had for resources. She was not a woman meant to be happy with mediocrity in any form. He wondered briefly if Gay had finally tumbled to her sister's true nature. There had been a wall between the two sisters too blatant to be missed. Eve was hurt, but beneath the pain, anger simmered and roiled. Sloane wasn't even certain Eve was aware of the caldron. Before the evening was over, he meant to dip a finger in that boiling pot. He might get burned, but he wouldn't be alone. Eve would be right there with him.

NINE

"Why don't you lean your head back and relax. You're so tense you'll crack if you don't ease up," Sloane suggested, glancing at Eve. The flickering streetlights created a strobe effect in the car, freezing expressions in space for a blink of an eye.

"I'm not usually like this," Eve said quietly, trying to do as he said. It was impossible. She couldn't forget Gay's words. Saint Eve's largess. If she had been able to hear it she was sure there would have been the slash of sarcasm to go with the terrible phrase. She had hurt Gay and hadn't even known she was doing it. She linked her hands together, squeezing to the point of pain.

Sloane caught the gesture out of the corner of his eye. He took one hand off the wheel and spread his fingers over hers. When she looked at him, he commanded, "Stop it. Just hang on for a few more minutes. We're almost there. Then I'll hold you and you can tell me what's wrong."

"I don't want to talk about it."

"You're not a liar."

"You can't help."

"You won't know that until I try."

Eve looked down at their hands, thinking of his strength, the way he had with the kids at Beginning Now. She could understand why they responded to him so well. He demanded honesty even when a person didn't want to give it because it hurt too much.

Sloane frowned at the way she sat, staring at his hand as though it were a lifeline. If Gay had been standing in front of him he would have damned her for whatever she had done to Eve. Instead, he concentrated on the deteriorating road that was the final leg of his journey. Suddenly, his headlights picked out the low wood building that seemed to rise gently from the hill on which it sat.

Eve glanced up as the bumps grew larger and the darkness more complete. A shadow, too perfectly straight-lined to be natural, materialized out of the trees. The headlights picked out the details of the structure, the native stone, the flash of glass for wide windows and softer reflection of wood formed to mate with the land rather than dominate it. "It looks like it belongs here," she said quietly, aware of the peacefulness of the setting even though it couldn't reach through her own disquiet to touch her soul.

Sloane pulled to a stop in the drive and switched off the engine. "Yancy's an architect. He designed the house for his wife."

"Lucky lady."

Sloane slipped out of his seat belt as he stared at

the house. "No. Not lucky at all. She died. She was in a car accident coming out here one day. She was six months pregnant. By the time someone found them, it was too late to save her or the baby."

Eve squeezed the hand she still held, for a moment taken out of her own misery to think of someone else's problem. She threaded her fingers between his clenched ones. "He grieves?"

"He's dying inside," he corrected, looking at her. "He won't come out here. She loved this place and spent every moment she could out here alone and with him. Some of his happiest memories are tied up in this one building. And he hates it."

"It hurts him to love it again."

"Love does hurt."

"Yes." She thought of Gay and what her family had suffered in spite of her efforts to protect them. Her parents still carried the guilt of what-if for not being omniscient enough to know a common childhood illness could steal her hearing. Her sisters and brother held a different kind of guilt for being able to hear when she could not. Each tried not to smother and a large portion of the time succeeded. But nothing took away that soul-destroying guilt. She had tried. She had hidden her fears, swallowed her rage, and caged her frustration for all the things that happened to her and for all the things she couldn't do. She had drawn a picture of herself that they needed, but she had also added colors, emotions, and needs that made them feel as though she had not lost so very much after all. It had been a gift of her love. An acknowledgment of theirs for her. Or so she had thought. With a few harsh words, Gay had made her question her choices.

"Talk to me, Eve," Sloane said. When she didn't answer, he touched her cheek, demanding she focus on his face rather than look through him to something so bleak that he couldn't stand to watch her. "Let's go inside." He tugged on her hand, pulling her gently across the seat so that she could get out on his side.

Neither spoke as they entered the cabin that was more a home in the woods than anything so rustic as a rural retreat. The walls were soft cream with wood molding and detailing. The furniture was jewel bright, clear colors of a rainbow, and ranged before a wide, welcoming hearth of river rock. The effect was a banquet to the senses. Herbs hung from the exposed beams, scenting the air so that the outdoors whispered to every corner.

"I'll start a fire. Yancy left a bottle of wine in the refrigerator. It was there the last time I came."

"I'll get it."

Sloane watched Eve head for the kitchen then he started a blaze with the tinder and logs laid ready for the flame. When it was burning to his satisfaction, he joined Eve on the couch. The wine was poured but he made no move to pick up one of the glasses from the tray on the table in front of him.

Eve could feel him waiting for an explanation. The need to pretend everything was fine was strong. She had spent too many years perfecting that skill not to want to take refuge in the strategy now. As if he could sense what she wanted to do she felt his hand on hers. She looked up into dark eyes that saw too much. Where there had been a wall between them now existed a communication she had never had with anyone else.

"Don't hide. Not from me. You don't need to."

"How did you know?" Her family had never guessed what she was doing.

"I didn't at first. But after watching you with Gay, seeing you at that faculty party, certain things didn't add up. No matter how stupid anyone around you was about your deafness, you always took it in stride. No sarcasm, no anger, no irritation. Nothing. Just calm acceptance as though inane comments, being patronized, and pity were a fact of your life. That just didn't fit with a woman with your kind of courage and drive."

"She called me Saint Eve."

He could tell there was a lot more to the problem than just the name, but the appellation was as good a starting point as any. "And it hurt?"

Eve hesitated, then spoke more harshly than she knew. "Yes, it hurt. A lot." Her breath came out in a gust of pain. "She has said it before, but I thought she was teasing."

"She might have been."

"She wasn't tonight," she said flatly, angrily. The emotions were tearing at her. She wanted to yell, to demand Gay take back what she said. The wish was useless. As useless as wishing for her hearing. Words spoken were seldom forgotten. Forgiveness was possible, but amnesia rarely happened but between the covers of a book. "I hate that name." She thrust her fingers together, her hands shaking with anger that she wanted to control and couldn't. Every word was making it that much harder to be calm. She took a deep breath, focusing on Sloane, praying he would help her back down before she couldn't.

"Don't fight it, Eve. Let it out before it eats you up." He shook her once, hard enough to demand she listen. "Stop bottling up whatever it is that makes you become Saint Eve. You're a whole woman. You told me so and you've proved it to everyone around you. Stop trying for canonization."

The push was enough. The anger broke gloriously free. Her eyes flashed with fire that Sloane had only seen in desire. She yanked out of his hold, glaring as she never had. Serenity had never been farther away. Peace was a forgotten dream. "Damn you, you have no right. You don't know one thing about any of this."

He faced her anger as he had their passion. Walking away was no longer an option of any kind. "Then tell me if you dare. Make it make sense, or are you afraid?"

The challenge sizzled between them. She went rigid with the demand that no one had ever made. His strength against hers. His power to her own. She inhaled, fighting him, reaching deeper into herself than she ever had before. "I am not afraid," she pushed out furiously, her hair flying with every high-mettled toss of her head.

Sloane wanted to kiss her senseless. He wanted to trap her fire long enough to brand them both with the flame. He caged his need to give to hers. "Then quit light-footing it around the problem and tell me the rest of what happened between you and your sister and why it is so damn important to you."

Eve surged to her feet, unable to sit still any longer. "Important!" she all but shouted, taking a jerky turn in front of him. "Do you have any idea what it's like to live with guilt and love as your constant shadows? My parents think they made me like this because they didn't see into the future enough to realize that something as simple as a rash and a long, high fever would have a permanent effect. My sisters and brother had to grow up compensating for my . . ." She paused then spit the word. ". . . handicap until I could learn how to cope on my own. Even then it wasn't enough. There was always some new kid to tease me about my deafness. Always some reason to defend me or take care of me. They didn't smother. They were stronger than that, but I knew what it was costing them to love me. So I tried." She wrapped her arms around herself. "God, how I tried to be perfect so they wouldn't have to apologize or defend. So they wouldn't have to feel guilty for what I was, I became more than I would have been as a hearing woman. At first I didn't even know what I was doing. I just knew it hurt to see what they did for me and what I never seemed to be able to do in return." She faced him, her eyes unknowingly pleading with him. "It was the only way to pay them back for caring for me." Tears filled her vision, sliding down her pale skin. She didn't wipe the moisture away. It didn't matter if Sloane saw her now. He had given her his truth. Now it was her turn.

Sloane came to his feet, wrapping his arms around her. There was a time for words. It would be later. Now he would hold her and let the pain wash away in her tears. Eve leaned into him, feeling him take her weight. She cried against his chest, unaware of the moment when he lifted her in his arms and carried her to the bed at the back of the house. The room was quiet, a haven. She curled into his warmth and let the memories and images of the past ebb and flow. She cried until she was dry, her fingers clenched in his shirt, her senses filled with his scent. There was no tomorrow, no yesterday. Only now mattered.

Sloane held her, frowning into the shadows. He thought of his own life and what it could have been like if he had shared his sterility with his family. When it had come time for children, wouldn't his brothers have been touched by the guilt that Eve's people had known? His father. His decision to keep his problem hidden had been motivated by his own needs, but in the end, he had protected them as well. But as he held Eve close he faced even more. He had denied them as well. Just as Eve had in reverse. Everyone had a right to feel. No one had the right to take that away just because it was uncomfortable. He had to tell his brothers and maybe his father. He wasn't ready yet, but there would be a time soon.

He stroked the hair back from her face, kissing her heated flesh. "Enough. You'll make yourself ill," he whispered against her temple. She wouldn't recognize the words, but she would know he was speaking to her by the movement of his mouth against her skin.

Eve sniffed inelegantly, then lifted her head. Her eyes were puffy, pink, her cheeks flushed. "What did you say?"

"I said, *enough*." He traced a last tear as it leaked from her lashes down her cheek. "Making yourself ill won't change a thing." He pulled a handkerchief from his pocket and dabbed up the moisture.

"I know." She raised her chin, finding his caring after the storm of grief and pain just what she needed. His tenderness carried no taint of guilt or responsibility. "But what *do* I do?"

"Pick up the pieces as you've always done." He tossed the handkerchief on the bedside table and pulled her into his arms once more, positioning her so she could read his lips.

"I don't know how." She shook her head in frustration. "I don't know how to be anything but what I was."

"Then learn something new. I am. You've taught me that much already. Save the good and change the rest of Saint Eve. She's worth the effort."

She searched his eyes, looking for and finding the truth. "Do you really believe that?"

"Yes. I won't lie to you, ever. I can't."

"Why?"

"Because I love you."

She blinked, certain she hadn't read those words. Sloane was no less surprised than she. But once the declaration was made, he didn't regret it. The love had been there almost from the first, but he had just been too stubborn to acknowledge it.

"You're sure?"

He nodded, smiling faintly at both her reaction and his own. He hadn't known it would be this easy to say. He touched her lips. His mouth straightened, no humor now. Only gravity that would change the words to something less than could be and more than had been. "I cannot take more than this from you. For as long as you want me, I'll share with you. But no more." He caressed the velvet skin marked by her tears and new self-knowledge. "No matter what you feel now or in the future, this is all there will ever be."

"Because of the child you cannot give me?"

"Yes."

"And if I love you? If I can tell you it doesn't matter to me and will never matter to me?"

"No difference. It matters to *me*. I told you why. I will not steal your right to have a child of your own body. I would give my soul to give you the seed of my blood. I cannot." For the first time in his life the words weren't acid on his tongue, a well-hidden secret never to know the light of day. Another gift from the woman called Eve. His mouth covered hers, the time for speaking with words done.

Eve felt his passion pour into his kiss, heating her own, reminding her that she had given herself to him. Later, she would consider the future he would not allow, the future she thought she needed. For now, she would take this moment with all the passion and joy that he had shown her existed. Pulling him close, she absorbed his weight and heat, warming herself in the fire and the desire. She gasped softly when his lips traced the top of each of her breasts. His kiss drifted over her, light as flower petals, giving pleasure with every touch. He slipped the bodice from her shoulders, then the dress down her hips and off. Her bra was flesh lace over satin skin. Her panties the same lace over light curls that guarded the secret of woman from man's eyes. A forefinger rimmed the border of each wisp of fabric, teasing her with every stroke until she writhed in an agony of wanting. His lips followed the path of his fingers, bringing more tension, more need. She moaned deep in her throat, arching to his mouth, his touch. She called his name and didn't know he answered, for her eyes were shut to all but the sensation of his impending possession. When she felt the lick of the room's coolness on her suddenly bare skin, she was past feeling any shock. She pulled him to her, her hands scoring his back in her need to complete what had begun in the sunlight of this day.

Sloane rose above her, loving her as he had no woman before Eve. She had come to him in darkness and led him into the light. She had shown him innocence and trust stronger than his own cynicism and the memories of his reality. She had healed him, touched him with dreams that he had forgotten. She was Eve. And tonight she was his by her choice and his.

"I think you are a rat, husband of mine," Pippa announced from the doorway of the bathroom that adjoined the master suite.

Josh glanced around, half out of his shirt. He eyed his wife for a moment, deciding if it was Pippa theatrics or truth creating the reaction. It was the first. That gleam in her eye had precious little to do with reality. "What have I done now?" he asked mildly, courting danger and the wicked retaliation that she was sure to aim in his direction and which he was just as certain to enjoy to the hilt.

Pippa sashayed to the center of the room, the negligee that he had bought her last Christmas caressing her bare skin with whisper-thin veils of pale pink. On another woman it would have been totally feminine. On Pippa it was dynamite.

"I have finally been able to figure out what you did. You set Sloane up with Eve Noble. It took a lot of finesse to find that out without calling Sloane and asking him outright if he had suddenly met a woman who mattered," she announced, yanking out her own rabbit from the marital hat. Josh didn't even blink at the revelation. Pippa sighed and wandered over to him, no nice intent in her eyes. "Do you have any idea how long it took me to find out what was going on?"

Josh checked his watch. "Give or take a minute. One month, three days, fourteen hours, and seven minutes." He pulled her close, laughing at her glare.

"You timed me," she accused, hardly able to believe it.

He inclined his head, his eyes daring her to do her damnedest. "I did," he admitted without remorse.

"I am going to get you for this."

He bent and lifted her in his arms. He walked the few feet to the bed and dropped her in the middle of it. "I certainly hope so," he agreed, watching her bounce twice before he came down beside her.

Pippa took his weight, her mind already busy with various, uniquely Pippa ways of evening the score. Josh read her expression with ease and held the other half of his secret silent. He wondered how long it would take for her to figure the whole.

TEN

The fire burned low in the grate, casting gentle shadows over the room. Eve lay in Sloane's arms amid the cushions he had pulled off the couch to make a place for them in front of the blaze. She picked up the glass of wine at her side and sipped the last few drops. "I like the place you found for us," she murmured softly. She turned so that she could see his face.

Sloane stroked her hair back, tucking it behind her ears. "I couldn't see us waltzing past Mike at my house or Gay at the guest house and explaining that we wanted to make love. And a motel didn't appeal at all."

He looked around the room, remembering the happiness that this retreat had seen. He glanced back at Eve. "I almost didn't bring you here."

"Because of your friend's tragedy?"

He nodded.

"It's hard not to feel guilty."

151

"Yes," he sighed. "Yance had it all. It's things like that which make you rail at fate."

"A waste of time. Every thing has its season whether we want to believe that or not. Your friend had more than a lot of people. The pain scores deep and it can cripple if he lets it. But it can also create something really wonderful as well. It's a matter of view and willingness to turn the pages of your own book of destiny."

"Sometimes a man can't turn those pages."

"He *won't* turn those pages," she corrected. She covered his mouth when he would have protested. "Everyone has a choice. As long as a person draws a breath he has a choice. He can fool himself into thinking he doesn't. He can create any number of excuses out of circumstances, lack of strength, resources or whatever, but the truth is that everyone of us does exactly what we want to do at any given time."

Sloane pulled her hand from his mouth, meeting her eyes. His gaze was no longer tender. "I won't change my mind, Eve."

Eve hesitated. It would be easy to back down, to take what he would give and hope that the physical attraction that was growing ever stronger would be enough to destroy the barrier he had forced between them. She loved him. The knowledge hadn't come in a blinding flash although she could remember the first time she had used the word in her mind. But even that could have been a long time after the impact of the emotion.

"I love you," she said softly, no longer hiding

behind the question of what-if. She watched him freeze, take the words as invisible blows.

Sloane stared at her eyes, reading truth where he would have preferred lies.

"I want to spend my life with you."

Still he said nothing.

Eve ached to reach out to him. The bleakness was back in his eyes, intensifying with every declaration she made. If she had any mercy for either of them, she would have swallowed her emotions, locked them away, and pretended that sex was enough. But she couldn't. She had spent too many years protecting those she loved that way. Sloane and she deserved more than a glass-case emotion. She would give him honesty, truth without evasion. And words were the only weapon she had to fight for their future. She wouldn't give in even to spare them this.

"I want to make a home and family with you."

That unlocked his muscles and the denial. "Damn you! I warned you."

"I didn't listen. I won't accept that this . . ." Her hand moved in a short arc to encompass their nakedness and their closeness. ". . . is all there is."

"You want children."

"We'll have them. We'll choose them together."

Sloane put her away from him. "No." He looked to the dying fire. "I won't let you make that kind of sacrifice."

"Why?" She sat up, not touching him, not worried that she wouldn't see his face or hear him. He was saying nothing she wanted to hear. "You accept me as I am. Why can't I do the same for you? Am I so fragile? So lacking in strength that I can't live with you day after day knowing my womb will be empty of your child? Is that what you're afraid of? That I will learn to hate and resent you and your sterility and forget to love?''

His head snapped around. Rage was a firestorm of emotion that had no outlet but vehemence. ''Yes, damn you. That's what I'm afraid of. I won't watch it happen. I won't hold on to heaven and feel it turn into hell.''

Eve didn't think. Her hand came up and she slapped him hard enough to make her palm sting. ''Damn you.'' She shook with temper and love. ''You condemn us both for such a flimsy excuse. You don't know me at all. Or are you giving me a picture of yourself? Will you one day grow to resent the fact that I can't hear you unless I'm looking at you?''

His face hurt, but he didn't notice. Her pain was deeper, more damaging. He got to his knees in one swift movement and caught her shoulders, shaking her hard enough to snap her head once. ''Don't you ever say that to me.''

She glared at him through the rain of her silken hair.

''I love you. I don't care what you can't do.''

''I feel the same.''

The challenge. Neither moved. The sound of their labored breathing was harsh in the silence of the war that had to be resolved. There could be no armistice. It was all or nothing.

''You can't guarantee a future.''

''Neither can you.'' Eve waited, holding her breath and knowing it.

Sloane searched her eyes, hoping, wishing, and knowing that he couldn't deny either of them any longer. "If there is even one doubt, tell me now. When I take you this next time there won't be any going back for either of us. If you try to leave me I won't let you go."

Her smile was shaky, relief and the last remnants of fear stealing its strength. "I will chain you to me any way I can. Every way I can." Her hands slipped up his chest, tracing his muscles, the hard body that could please her as no other. "You are mine. I've been alone and now I'm not. If you think I'm going to let anything take that from me, you didn't read that book as well as you thought you did."

He pulled her close, his relief too great to be as gentle as he would have liked. "I read it very well. For a while I fooled myself enough to let you get close. I set my own trap, it seems. Because I was certainly warned that you have the devil's own determination."

Eve laughed, joy coming out of hiding to color her expression, to light her eyes. "Who me? Saint Eve?"

Sloane covered her laughing mouth. "To hell with Saint Eve," he decreed when he raised his head. "I know a disguise when I see one."

"You know you never did ask me to marry you," Eve murmured as Sloane drove them home. She shifted in her seat, feeling a number of little twinges that went with very thorough loving. The satisfied curve of her lips was as old as woman's first wile.

Sloane glanced at her, one brow raised. Her look

was cat-in-the-cream smug. If he hadn't been driving, he would have taken great pleasure in tasting that smile. "I warned you about changing your mind."

Eve ignored the goad as beneath her notice. She had other ways of teasing her man. "I thought a huge splashy wedding would be nice. My family will love it, and from what you tell me about how your brothers got their wives, your family will like the idea, too."

Sloane's mood changed in a heartbeat. He studied her for a second trying to decide if she was joking. Her innocent look was too well done not to be real from a woman who didn't seem to have a feminine trick to her name. "Wouldn't you like a family affair instead?" he asked carefully, trying not to remember the few times he had been stuffed into a morning suit as best man for friends. The confusion. The rounds of parties. The lack of privacy. The jokes. His memory was apparently better than he had realized.

Eve hid a grin. The limited light definitely didn't do Sloane's reluctant *this-is-going-to-kill-me-but-I'll-do-it-because-I-love-you* expression justice. "It will be our only marriage and the first for both of us."

Sloane bit back a groan.

"Think of all your colleagues. I'll bet most of your students will want to attend."

He did groan then.

Eve couldn't stop the laughter.

Sloane knew when he had been outgunned. "Honey, you have just sealed your fate. I'm going to tell my father this morning that we're engaged. You think that big-wedding idea was a joke, but he'll make anything you could think up to tease me look small-time. He knows half the eastern seaboard. We'll be lucky to find a church to hold the influx.''

Eve's laughter died. "You wouldn't.''

His teeth flashed with his grin as he pulled into his driveway instead of hers. He didn't immediately notice the excess of cars parked on the street in front as he turned to her, stripped her out of the seat belt, and pulled her onto his lap. If she hadn't been so tiny, the maneuver never would have worked. "You might as well tell your mother and father to make a list.''

"I didn't mean it.'' Eve had her own visions of the kind of circus a big wedding would be. "You know I didn't mean it.''

"Male honor, woman. You keep challenging me. I don't want to turn into a wimp,'' he whispered before nipping gently at her ear.

"You couldn't be a wimp if you tried.'' She tilted her head to give him better access.

Sloane indulged himself, even as he silently cursed the public setting. Necking in his own car in the driveway was not the image of the college professor. But then, who wanted to be that staid male anyway? He took her lips and heated the snug confines with a dash of passion. He stroked her breasts, the fabric barrier becoming a stimulant as well as a veil of modesty.

Eve's soft gasp echoed his own moan of need. He raised his head and forced his breathing to slow, his body to remember there was a bed a few yards away and dawn was close. "How do you feel about champagne and eggs?"

"I'm hungry enough to eat anything," she answered honestly as he opened his door and slid out with her in his arms. "Do you realize you do a lot of carrying me around?"

"That's because you fit so nicely right here." He hugged her once and then set her reluctantly on her feet. Keeping her hand in his, he started up the walk. Then he noticed the cars. He stopped, staring at one of the shapes. "If I didn't know that Slater is supposed to be in California on a case, I would swear that's Joy's Blazer."

"Your brother Slater?" Eve peered past him. "You said he was coming to visit."

Sloane thrust the key into the front door lock. "The plan was still in the talking stage the last I heard."

"Is that a problem?" Eve followed Sloane into the hallway, which was lit by one light.

"Normally, no. The house has four bedrooms. Exactly enough for the whole clan at one time. It's one of the reasons I bought the place." He led the way to the kitchen, frowning at the light he could see coming from that direction. "Mike must be up." Just as he finished the sentence he rounded the corner to find the midsize area filled with males.

"Well, you finally make it home, middle brother," Slater drawled, eyeing Eve with interest. He was sprawled in one chair, his legs stretched out in front of him. There was a day's growth of beard on his handsome face and his clothes looked as though he had been rolling around in them.

"It looks like we managed to surprise him again," Stryker observed from where he leaned against the counter, on which resided a coffeepot only half full. One lean hand was wrapped around Sloane's favorite mug. Every hair was in place. No stubble marked his face and his clothes looked as though they had just left his perfectly kept closet. He was sleek, *GQ* groomed, and the exact clone of Sloane and Slater in features, build, and coloring.

"I forgot to tell you that Slater was calling to say they were coming in tonight," Mike muttered from his place in one of the other chairs at the table.

Sloane glared at his parent, both of them knowing the older man had bent the truth out of all recognition.

Mike glared back.

Eve tried to stifle her amusement at the looks flying about the room. She was getting more than a cursory glance from both brothers. As for herself, it was somewhat disconcerting to be facing exact duplicates of the man she loved. Even the eyes were the same. If they were dressed alike, she wasn't sure she'd know Sloane at all.

"I told you we would find them in the kitchen."

At the sound of his wife's voice, Stryker looked at his watch. "I told you she wouldn't sleep past dawn. Pregnant or not, that woman gets up before the sun."

"I don't like this hour of the morning at all," Tempest muttered. "At least not right now." She patted her rounded belly as she and Joy entered the kitchen to find their spouses wrapped around life-giving coffee that Tempest had given up for the duration. "The least you could do is drink tea while I'm in this condition," Tempest grumbled sleepily. She paused on her way to her husband long enough to give Sloane's arm a pat and the slender woman beside him a sharp look out of half-closed eyes. Then she walked into Stryker's arms. "You promised me morning sickness would only last three months."

Stryker hugged her close before reaching behind him for the cup of tea he had just finished making before Sloane and Eve had come in. He poked the cup under his disgruntled wife's nose. "Wrap your mouth around that, my love."

She made a face. "I hate tea."

Joy sat down on her husband's lap and tried to suppress a laugh. She turned her head so that Eve could read her lips. Mike had explained about Eve and her sister. He had also hinted at a romance brewing. Slater and Stryker had been ready to believe their father. She hadn't been so certain. Now, after having seen the two together, she was prepared to change her mind. They looked as though they belonged to each other. "You're going to think you've fallen into a nest of nuts."

"I heard that," Tempest mumbled, sipping and willing her stomach to remember it hated tossing up meals at the first sign of movement.

Eve shot a quick, searching glance at Sloane's face, trying to gauge how this talk of impending parenthood was affecting him. The pleased look he made no effort to hide denied her concern. "Rough pregnancy?"

"I'm a baby," Tempest announced before draining the last of her tea. The brew had put some stiffening back in her spine, a bit of energy in her limbs, and calmed her gastric seas. "I hate being sick, and this little bundle of mischief is driving me nuts," she added, patting her stomach. She grinned at Eve. "But I only have five more months to go, so it could be worse." She leaned back so that Stryker was her pillar of balance. "Did they introduce themselves?" She sent a quick look around, catching the surprise on the male faces. "Idiots. They didn't."

"I'm Tempest. This is Stryker. That's Slater and Joy."

"Eve Noble." Eve returned the compliment. There was something likable about the woman called Tempest that denied the word *stranger*. The one called Joy was more cautious, not pretty at all, but there was a kind of strength in her face that said no problem, no obstacle was too great to be handled.

Tempest grinned engagingly. "We know. Mike's been singing your and your sister's praises. Although, if I'm being accurate, your sister figured in the conversation a little more than you. Finally, he has someone he can drag in and out of the bargain barns he loves so much. I don't suppose anyone remembered to find you a chair, either. Or get you a cup of coffee." She turned her head, frowning up at her husband. "I thought you had manners."

"Not my woman."

Chuckling at Stryker's swift denial of responsibility, Sloane urged Eve toward a vacant chair.

"You want coffee or tea?" Mike asked, starting to get up.

"We thought champagne," Sloane said, watching Eve's face rather than the reactions of his relatives.

He winked when she smiled mischievously up at him.

Eve scanned the sea of soon-to-be-family faces, laughing aloud at the various responses. Today, all things were possible and everything had an element of joy.

"Champagne?" Mike blinked at his son, for once in his life at a loss for words.

Not so for Tempest. "You're getting married," she announced, the gray funk of pregnancy giving way to excitement. Her eyes lit with enthusiasm.

Stryker could feel the energy coursing through her. "Calm down, my storm, before you pop." He caught her before she could launch herself at Sloane.

Slater looked Sloane over, reading the pride and love in dark eyes so like his own. The woman at his side looked perfect. He could understand the feeling, he decided, sliding his fingers through Joy's and raising his wife's hand to his lips. Her smile was the same as his, pleased with the newest member of the clan, Sloane's choice.

"Well, I'll be damned," Mike said finally, sitting back down and staring at the pair. "I was hoping." He ignored the three male snorts of derision from his offspring. "But I didn't really believe it."

"It's nice to know I sneaked this one by you," Sloane replied with a grin, realizing no one was going to break out the bottle of champagne. He wandered to the refrigerator while Eve fielded the questions coming fast and furious about their plans.

"Sloane doesn't want a big event and neither do I," Eve said when Tempest demanded the privilege of planning the wedding. "Family only."

"And a few special friends," Tempest urged. "That will only make it at least forty on Sloane's side."

Eve's brows rose. "Forty?"

Sloane turned, bottle in hand. "You're looking a little green," he murmured, unable to resist teasing her.

"There are at least that many on my side when you count all the cousins and so forth."

Tempest brushed past Sloane to rummage in the drawer where he kept his writing supplies for the odd kitchen list. Paper and pen in hand, she plopped into one of the chairs at the table and began scribbling. Joy collected the flutes for the champagne. Slater found a couple of extra chairs from the dining room and brought them in.

"If Tempest is determined to attack this now, we'd better plan on breakfast," Sloane said, rolling up his shirtsleeves. He went to a cabinet and pulled out three skillets. "Mike, you get the eggs. Joy, you might find some orange juice to go with the champagne since I'm sure Stryker is going to nix the sauce for his storm."

Eve stared at the mass confusion that was sorting itself into an impromptu wedding planning party. Suddenly she thought of Gay. "I have to call my sister. She doesn't even know yet."

"I'll pick her up for you," Slater offered as he passed with the last chairs dangling from two lean hands.

"How does she like her eggs?" Stryker demanded from the stove as he took over one of the frying pans.

"Over medium," Eve answered automatically, then laughed. No one even noticed that she was feeling as though the entire clan had sprouted wings and flown. Apparently she wasn't going to be allowed to be a stranger invading their midst.

Sloane poured her a glass of bubbly and kissed her lightly. "I should have warned you."

She shook her head, liking his family almost as much as she loved him. Other than to make certain that they faced her when they spoke, they seemed completely unaware of her deafness. She was Sloane's fiancée, a part of him and therefore someone they were prepared to accept and like. She had never known such openheartedness. "It's much better this way," she assured him. "They have to be experienced to be appreciated."

Dawn crept gently into the bedroom, bathing the two entwined figures sleeping so peacefully in morning light. Josh's face was strong even in repose and Pippa's had a fallen angel's mystique. Suddenly, the insistent ring of the phone beside the bed stole the last moments of slumber. Pippa muttered a curse and tried to tuck her head under Josh's shoulder to blot out the sound. Josh groped for the receiver as he pushed himself erect. Grinning sleepily at his wife's grumbles, he patted her bare bottom before dropping his pillow over her head.

"Luck," he said reflexively as he cradled the phone to his ear.

"You're up," Mike boomed.

Josh winced and glanced quickly at the clock beside his shoulder on the table. "Not usually at six," he replied dryly. The tone of Mike's voice was not the kind to indicate trouble. "Why am I up at this hour?" He stroked Pippa's uncovered back, enjoying the quiver of response that was strong enough to reach past the veils of sleep.

"Because you pulled it off when I didn't think you could. Beat that wife of yours, too."

That got Josh's wandering attention. "Sloane? And Eve?"

Pippa's head popped out from under the pillow, her eyes surprisingly alert.

"You did it," Mike crowed. "They're getting married, and you and your group will get an invitation. You said you could do it."

Josh grinned at the older man's exuberance. "Beginner's luck."

Mike snorted. "More like living with that Pippa."

Since he didn't modulate his voice, the remark was heard by Pippa. She snatched the phone from her laughing spouse . . . she'd deal with him later . . . and entered the fray. "I heard that."

"Don't care if you did, woman. That was a smart move your man made. I always give the devil his due. And he beat you out on this one. You said you couldn't find my boy a mate."

"It's still in the family," she reminded him.

Mike roared with laughter. "You can say that again." The sounds of the party drifted up to his room. "Gotta go before Sloane finds out that I'm calling you. He'd have my ears and tail, for sure."

The moment Mike hung up, Pippa passed the phone to Josh. His smug look proclaimed some very irritating moments in her future. "I suppose you're going to live on this for months."

Josh considered the idea. "No. More like years." His eyes dared her to deny him the right.

She tried not to be amused at the way he had turned the tables on her. Her lips twitched, then steadied.

"You won't be able to hold it in forever," he murmured, daring her to keep a straight face.

"I'll make a recovery."

"Maybe. But then I might just pull off another coup," he goaded, thinking of the other half of his great plan.

Pippa's eyes narrowed. Being bested once might be livable. Twice wasn't even on the list. "Want to bet?"

His look sharpened at the challenge. With Pippa, those were some of his favorite words. "What?"

"I want to learn to fly."

"Over my dead body."

For the moment, she ignored that intriguing possibility. "I think a little pink plane might be nice. Something racy. My name on the side." She rolled onto his chest, wriggling into her favorite position as she nipped gently at one nipple. The ripple the tiny caress brought pleased her.

Josh caught her shoulders, lifting her up so that he wasn't distracted by her touch. "You're making a blind bet."

"I have faith in chance. Once, you might be able to pull off but not twice."

He thought that over. The second half of his idea was a lot more risky in many ways than the first.

Common sense said he should back out with what little of his dignity he could. But common sense and Pippa didn't even exist in the same world. "All right. But I pick out the instructor."

"Preparing to lose?" Her fingers danced over his chest, teasing him.

"Covering my tail is more like it," he muttered, giving up on the idea of not being distracted. He liked the diversion too much to be that stupid. "We should get up at dawn more often," he added huskily, pulling her tight against him and then rolling her over so that she was trapped under his body.

She laughed up at him. "Makes you amorous, does it?"

"Something like that," he agreed before silencing her in the only effective way he had ever found.

ELEVEN

Eve sat back and watched the family gathered around the table. The love that flowed between the various members was undisguised. The marriages that had been made were very different but equally strong. Stryker was protective of his dare-anything wife, his care subtle, clearly geared to guard without stifling Tempest's need to fly on her own. Slater seemed joined with his Joy in some way that Eve still couldn't define even after the last few hours of study. They didn't touch each other as much as Stryker and Tempest or even she and Sloane, and yet there was no way to miss the communication that seemed to be going on without them exchanging so much as a look. Intrigued, curious as to how Gay perceived her soon-to-be in-laws, she glanced at her sister where she sat beside Mike on the loveseat. The group had long since vacated the kitchen, after a breakfast that had turned into a celebration of the impending wedding and a friendly argument over where the ceremony would take place.

Sloane touched Eve's shoulder, drawing her eyes. "Happy?"

She nodded, forgetting Gay as she touched the man who loved her. "Very. But do you think we'll get to make any suggestions?" She inclined her head toward the six people huddled around the loveseat, most talking at once.

"Probably not. Besides, Tempest really is good at organizing things." He frowned slightly as he looked at his sister-in-law. Her belly was swollen visibly now. Eve would never know the fulfillment that Tempest would. Never feel her own child suckle at her breast. His hand tightened on her shoulder, regret for what could not be stealing the happiness from his expression for a moment.

Eve saw the change. "Don't."

He looked down at her, no longer feeling threatened by what she could see. "I can't forget."

"I'm not asking you to. But you don't need to keep beating yourself with it. I love you and I will miss having your babies. But not enough to risk spending my life without you in it. There is no price I wouldn't pay for that." If she loved him enough, if she kept reminding him of that love, maybe one day he would heal enough to accept without regret.

He leaned down, needing to taste those words from her mouth. Cupping the back of her head, he took what she gave willingly. "I love you," he whispered when he raised his head.

"Break it up, you two," Mike called from across the room. "This is your wedding, and if you don't get over here and make your presence felt, Tempest is going to have Eve marching down the aisle behind a bunch of bridesmaids that no one, including me, has ever heard of. And I can't see Jay, Jr., standing still long enough to be a ring bearer even for Josh. More than likely, the kid will be swinging from a tree or something.''

Sloane grinned, the dark mood forced away by Eve's declaration. It would be back, but he would remember what she had said. It would be his talisman. "Come on. If Tempest is talking about Jay, Jr., in this wedding we are in real trouble."

Eve rose. "Who is Jay, Jr.?"

Joy heard the question. "A limb of a she-devil named Pippa. He looks like an angel and has the ingenuity of a Houdini."

Eve sat down in the spot that Tempest had made for her on the couch Stryker had drawn close to the loveseat. "Who's Pippa?"

The sudden silence impressed all the occupants except Eve. She was only aware of the identical expressions of blank shock on all the faces around her, Sloane's included. Tempest was the first to recover. She patted Eve's hand. "Believe me, if we started on who and what Pippa is, you wouldn't be married in this decade." She frowned thoughtfully. "Or maybe even the next."

Sloane dropped onto the floor at Eve's feet, angling his body so she could see his face. "Trust us, the best way to appreciate Pippa is to meet her."

Joy took pity on Eve's bewildered expression. "Pippa is a matchmaker. One way or another she is responsible for Slater and me finding each other and for Stryker and Tempest getting together."

"I arranged that myself," Stryker pointed out.

Joy gave him a straight look. "Right. I distinctly remember you telling me about that woman Pippa fixed you up with who matched your so-called perfect profile to the letter. Pippa warned both of you that it wouldn't work and she was right."

"That had nothing to do with Tempest."

Tempest jammed an unladylike elbow in her spouse's ribs. "You have a convenient memory. I had been dying of love for you for years. Pippa got you to see that you felt the same. Personally, I think she's great. I can't wait to see what she says when I tell her I want her as godmother to our daughter."

Stryker stared at his wife as though she had taken leave of her senses. "You wouldn't."

She nodded, patting her belly complacently. "I will." She glanced at Eve. "It's almost a tradition, at least for the ones Pippa has brought together. It's a shame you and Sloane won't be able to join the tradition. Joy and I really like the idea of being able to give Pippa a double whammy. A triple would be even better."

Eve felt Sloane stiffen against her legs. She wanted to cry out at the pain the innocent words caused him. But before she could do anything, Mike took the focus off her and Sloane.

"What do you mean, you and Joy?" He caught Joy's hand, touching her as he rarely did, even though he was a man who liked making a physical link with those who mattered to him. "Are you pregnant, daughter?"

Joy shrugged uncomfortably. It was still hard for her to accept the open affection the McGuire men offered her. Slater's touch soothed her enough to smile and mean it. "Yes. That's why we decided to descend on Sloane with Tempest and Stryker. We thought the announcement would be a good reason to have a party. Then Eve and Sloane stole our thunder." Her glance encompassed both.

Mike grinned, so pleased he felt like dancing in the streets. "Hot damn. Granddaddy times two." He eyed each woman in turn. "Or maybe times four," he added hopefully. "After all, you boys did get started on your families late."

"No, you don't," Stryker muttered, dropping an arm over his wife's shoulders. "There is only one baby in there." He stared at his wife, daring her to tell him differently. "Isn't there?"

Tempest's innocent look wasn't designed to reassure. Stryker swallowed hard.

Slater studied his wife, silently asking his own question. Her faint shrug was definitely not helpful. "Shut up, Mike," he grunted. Handling one baby was enough to start. He didn't want to think about the possibility of two.

Sloane watched the interplay, remembering Eve's words, holding on to them and to her hand. It was becoming more imperative by the moment to tell his brothers. Not because of *his* feelings, but her own. Every time someone mentioned the pregnancies or children, she felt his loss and pain. He hadn't thought a woman existed who could care for him so much that she could share his loss so completely. For now, all he could do was change the subject.

"As much as I like the idea of watching Pippa cope with your news, we had better make some decisions."

"Sloane's right," Slater seconded, ready to be diverted from the possibility his father had raised. "For one thing, if we intend to pull this off in the next two weeks . . ." He paused to grin at his brother. ". . . and remembering my own wish to get the legalities over with, I can understand the rush, we'd better get a plan together. There are certainly enough of us to divide the work."

"There is one thing we have to do," Gay said. She had let the arrangements roll over her, not because she wasn't interested, but because she wasn't certain how to help Eve. She couldn't forget she had hurt her sister when she had never intended to. She wouldn't risk that again.

"The house," Eve murmured.

"No, actually I was thinking about your clothes and mine. We only brought enough for a week, and while most of it will stretch, there isn't any reason why it should. Plus, if you don't mind," she offered hesitantly, "I could go home and personally handle any questions the family may have."

Eve considered the idea, seeing the faint pleading in Gay's eyes. Her sister needed to do something to help. Saint Eve would have jumped in, eager to reestablish their earlier relationship. This Eve understood that honesty was more important. "You wouldn't mind?"

Gay smiled with relief. "A little bit," she admitted. "But I won't be gone long. It's a short flight and I shouldn't have any trouble getting a plane out."

"Don't worry about that. You can use mine," Stryker suggested.

"And I'll go with you," Mike added. "Gotta meet my in-laws, you know."

Tempest rolled her eyes. "Gay, honey, you'd better make sure you warn your people."

Mike pseudoglared at his daredevil daughter. "You get rid of that maniac stallion of yours yet?" he shot back, restarting an old war between them. "It isn't the thing for a mother."

"I'm not a mother yet," Tempest retaliated, firing up.

"You didn't let her on that thing, Stryker?"

Sloane rose and pulled Eve to her feet. "If you two are going to go at it, Eve and I are disappearing. We'll be at her place if anyone comes to his senses," he announced over the fray that was heating up with every new voice.

"I don't think anyone heard you," Eve observed, watching in amazement as her sister took Mike's side against his son.

Sloane had already reached the same conclusion. There were times when he wondered if all families were as involved as his. "That means we can make a clean getaway." He urged her out of the room and down the hall. "With any luck, they won't know we're missing for hours."

She laughed as they stepped into the warmth of the sun. She hadn't been able to hear the noise and confusion, but she had certainly felt and imagined it. "I like them. All of them."

He turned her in his arms. It wouldn't have mattered if Eve hadn't taken to any of them or they to her. "I love you."

She stroked his face. "You'd better. You're stuck

with me now. You've given your word in front of witnesses."

"Best thing I ever did."

His kiss was passion under wraps but waiting for its moment to blossom. Eve drank of its essence, silently thanking the hand of fate that had decreed their worlds had merged long enough for passion to mature into love.

Tempest flopped down on the couch and stared irritably at the small stack of parcels lying drunkenly on the chair across the room. "I'm exhausted and that's all we have to show for one day of shopping. I've never worked so hard in my life with so little to show for it. Mountain climbing is easier."

Joy eyed the stack, then her sister-in-law. "You weren't carrying around two when you were mountain climbing," she pointed out, kicking off her shoes and propping her feet on the hassock in front of her chair.

"I could do with a cup of tea myself, but I don't think I have the energy to get up and make it," Eve added, curling her feet under her as she got comfortable on the other end of the couch from Tempest. "I don't know why I let the two of you talk me into going into every store in the tri-city area. I have enough stuff to wear to last a year and we still haven't found a dress for the ceremony."

"That's because you're so choosy," Tempest replied without rancor.

"I'm not that choosy! Didn't we get the florist order in, the cake picked out and ordered and a restaurant for the rehearsal dinner, and the wedding cel-

ebration in the first two days?'' The last week of
racing around getting ready to step in front of a min-
ister had been a whirlwind way to get to know her
soon-to-be relatives, both the males and females. She
liked them all, the different personalities, the ease
with which they adjusted to the needs of one another,
and their open caring. They accepted her, first because of Sloane and now, she realized, because she
filled a niche in the whole. She valued that niche,
found joy in the responsibility and warmth in the
need they had of her and what was growing in her
for them.

"She's got you there, Temp." Joy grinned at
Tempest's glare, then added to Eve, "Neither Tempest nor I had a regular wedding. It's only fair one
of the trips gets the real thing."

Eve grunted, something she had never done in her
life. "In other words, the only hope in the world I
have to find a dress that suits me is to leave you two
at home."

Tempest sat up, looking more alive than she had
a moment before. "You try leaving us out now, at
this late date, and Joy and I will haunt you." She
glanced at Joy. "Right?"

Joy nodded, her eyes dancing with mischief that
she had learned to express through her life with the
McGuire family. "Got it in one. We might even
have to think of a way to decorate the going-away
car."

"You wouldn't!" Eve shook her head, chuckling.
"I take that back. You *would*. All of you. Mike
probably leading the pack."

"Actually, I think it would be a three-way tie," Joy observed judiciously.

"No, Stryker would lead," Tempest said, pushing to her feet with a groan. "And that's only because Sloane wouldn't be in the game." She wandered toward the kitchen. "If you two want tea, get up and help."

Joy rose. "That woman never ceases to surprise me. She sees things that you wouldn't expect her to know the way she's always racing around, chasing the next thrill."

"I thought she had settled down. Or at least, I'm sure that's what Sloane told me."

"She did, but only in Tempest's fashion. For you or me that would be the equivalent of going over Niagara Falls in a barrel."

They entered the kitchen together.

"I've never done that," Tempest said, looking up as she filled the kettle.

Joy shook her head. "Don't even think it. So help me, I'll tell Stryker on you."

Tempest glared at her.

Joy glared back.

Eve watched the pair, trying not to laugh. "How old did you say you were?"

Tempest ignored the question. "The minute I get pregnant the whole world decides I need a keeper."

"Somebody has to give Stryker a hand."

Tempest popped the kettle down on the burner. "He does just fine by himself. Besides, wait until Slater starts hovering over you. It will drive you just as wild as it does me. Don't call me when it gets bad because I'm going to enjoy reminding you how little sympathy I got from you in my hour of need,'' she muttered righteously.

Joy rolled her eyes. "I didn't know theatrics went with the condition."

"Cute, Joy, cute."

Eve giggled. Both women turned to her, glaring. She covered her mouth, but nothing could hide her expression. "I can't help it," she explained. "The two of you have been going at it all day."

"We have not," Tempest denied without thinking.

Joy frowned, considering the charge. Sighing, she admitted, "She's right."

"Oh." Tempest folded her arms across her aching breasts. That was another bone she had to pick with this breeding business. "I suppose we should try for a little decorum."

Joy snorted. "Not in a million years for any of us."

"Don't even make the attempt. I can't remember the last time I've had so much fun. You can plan my wedding anytime."

Tempest shook her head. "No way. I don't think Sloane would thank us for helping you to get away from him enough to be contemplating this with anyone else. You only get one wedding and we intend to see that it is something special."

"Amen to that." Joy reached into the cabinet and pulled out three mugs. "Let's drink to the last marriage ceremony of the clan."

"Not quite the clan. Mike's still single."

Tempest poured hot water into each of their cups. "Always will be to hear him tell it."

"Maybe we ought to get this Pippa all of you told me about working on him," Eve suggested.

"He'd run a hundred miles to get out of her way," Joy replied, dunking her tea bag with the disgust of a real tea drinker faced with a bag instead of leaves. "Of course, Pippa would run him to ground and make him like being hunted."

"Everything you tell me about this woman is only whetting my curiosity."

The three ranged themselves around the table. "You'll meet her soon."

"And you'll like her whether you want to or not," Joy added. "She makes you think of every dangerous thing you know, and yet you have the feeling you could tell her the most important secret of your life and you would find safety and empathy in the sharing."

Eve sipped her tea, thinking of Sloane's secret, the pain that just looking at his brothers and their wives must cost him. "A special lady."

"Very special."

"Part witch woman," Tempest said, raising her mug to the catalyst to Joy's and her life. "I can't wait for you to meet her next week."

Sloane traced the outline of the dawn shadows over Eve's bare skin. This was one of his favorite parts of the day, these moments before his family intruded on their time. Eve had fit in so easily with Joy and Tempest. His brothers liked her. Her deafness had been accepted, allowed for but not dwelled on. He was proud of the woman he loved and those who loved him. And in a few more days the future would be a golden bridge of time. Only one shadow still lingered as he watched Joy and Tempest change with each day of their pregnancy. His brothers' care of their wives, their pride and pleasure in the natural cycle of life awoke envy that he had never had before. It ate at him, and no amount of rational thinking had succeeded in changing his futile wish that things could be different. He watched Eve share Joy and Tempest's delight in their condition and that hurt, too. She would never have that, not by his seed. He had thought himself past bitterness. It was difficult to admit to himself that he was not. He thought these days of artificial insemination. At least that way he could give Eve a child of her body if not of his blood.

Eve lay beside Sloane, feeling the slowly growing tension in his long frame. She could always tell when he was thinking about what would never be theirs. "You can't keep doing this to yourself," Eve whispered, sliding her hand over his chest to where his heart beat so steadily.

Sloane looked down at her, his fingers covering hers, pressing them against his skin. "I don't want you ever to regret what loving me has cost you."

Eve chose her words with care. She couldn't devalue what would never be, but she would never stop trying to make him see that he mattered more than anything he couldn't do. "The cost isn't greater than the joy you give me."

"I want you to have a child of your body," he said quietly, the idea taking root as he lay there, her bare flesh wedded to his. He slipped their linked hands to her empty womb. "There are ways."

"Artificial insemination."

His eyes held hers. "Yes."

She had wanted more than she could articulate to be able to give him the child that nature had denied his right to have. But not this way. A baby had to be made in love, for both of them. He wanted this child for her, a hostage against her feelings changing for him. The thought burned hot and deep into her mind. She could live with his sterility but not with his distrust of their future. Anger came swiftly, controlled, cold fire to match the pain. "Your inability to father a child will not be the thing that destroys us. It will be your lack of faith in my love. I can't live with this. I won't live with it. I won't pay some other woman's emotional bills. I am not marrying you for a child. I love you. Not your ability to father offspring." She pulled her hand away and slipped from the bed they shared, from his warmth, from the joy of his body.

Stunned at her reaction, Sloane rose quickly, cutting the distance between them to nothing. He grabbed her shoulders, holding her prisoner when she tried to pull away. "I want you to have your dreams. I hate knowing that I am stealing them."

"No one ever gets everything they want in life. We make do, and sometimes, if we're very lucky, we get far more than we ever gave up." She caught his troubled face in her hands. "I want your promise. This is the last time we ever mention this part of this subject again." She searched his eyes before she continued, spacing each word with care. "I choose to marry you knowing the truth. I accept our future as it stands now. I want you to do so as well."

"And if I can't?"

"Then you condemn us both to moments like this. Tainted happiness. Distrust. Pain."

Sloane understood what she was saying, what she was asking.

"Tell your brothers. Stop hiding this as though it were some fatal flaw."

Still he said nothing.

"Tell your father."

That loosened his tongue. He shook his head. "He'll blame himself. I can't do that to him."

Eve knew about guilt suffered by damaged children. "All right. But think about your brothers. Let them really know you, Sloane. They deserve that, and so do you. Maybe you can't be a biological father, but you can be one hell of an uncle and adoptive parent."

He hadn't thought he could smile. He discovered he was wrong as he listened to the unaccustomed curse on Eve's tongue. Her pronunciation was a little off because she hadn't learned the word during her hearing years but she got her point across. "My own Eve. I love you more than I will ever be able to tell you."

"You just keep on thinking like that and the rest is small change."

"Promise?"

She wrapped her arms around Sloane's neck and pulled his head down so that their lips were almost touching. "Promise."

TWELVE

Sloane propped his feet up on the desk and leaned back in his chair. His brothers were ranged around his study, each with a mug of coffee cupped in one hand. The house was devoid of female occupation as Joy and Tempest had hijacked Eve for the last round of shopping before what the male contingency had begun to term the "big event."

"I love my wife but how she can keep running in stores buying things is beyond me." Stryker shook his head, then took a swallow of caffeine.

"I know what you mean. I don't know what it is about this wedding, but Joy is more involved than I have ever seen her. I don't think there can be one more thing left to buy."

"The wedding dress," Sloane muttered.

Stryker ignored Sloane's comment. "It's Eve, not the wedding. The women really like her."

"Don't sound so surprised," Sloane said, eyeing his brother.

"I'm not surprised they like her. She's a very likable woman. I'm just surprised at how fast Joy and Tempest have taken to her."

"Eve's like that."

Slater nodded. "You picked well, brother."

Sloane looked down into his empty mug, thinking about Eve and all that she had brought to his life. And what she had asked of him. She was right whether he wanted to admit it or not. He had shortchanged his brothers in hiding so much of himself from them. They had always been there for him and he for them. It was past time he remembered that. The moment was now. He looked up to find twin faces staring at him as though they knew he had something to say.

"You might as well spit whatever it is out," Slater murmured.

"You've been looking like you can't decide which way to jump all morning," Stryker added bluntly when Sloane made no effort to speak.

Sloane put his mug on the edge of the desk, then sat up straight. "I'd like to spit it out, but this is one time when getting the words out is damn hard."

"You know you have our help no matter what the problem," Stryker said, setting his own cup aside.

"We're an unbeatable team," Slater agreed, the only one of them remaining in a lazy sprawl. His gaze was just as sharp, as clear, but he only moved when necessary and when he knew the direction.

The unquestioning support was no less than had always been, but this time it wouldn't carry the day as it had in the past. "This isn't something we can beat, singly or collectively."

Slater's eyes narrowed. Stryker tensed. Neither man said a word.

There was no easy way to lead into his confession, so Sloane didn't try. "I'm sterile."

Two curses, succinct, graphic, and vehement. The male horror. A man's pride and especially a McGuire's, whose pride and sense of family was bred soul-deep.

"How?" Stryker managed one word as he groped with the first problem in his life that had no visible solution. Only two other times in his life had he felt this helpless—watching Slater die and waiting for Tempest to fly away to her next life-threatening dare. He had won both those battles, through patience and loving. Neither would work here.

"A freak of a maniacal fate." Sloane shook his head and rose to pace to the window.

Slater's hands clenched around the mug he held until his fingers hurt. Carefully, watching his brother's rigid back, he set the mug aside. "How did you find out?"

Sloane didn't turn around. "Helen and I lived together for that year and she was trying to get pregnant although she didn't tell me. Finally, after ten months of trying she went to her doctor for fertility tests."

"I always said that woman was a nut. Lots of women don't conceive at the drop of a hat," Slater muttered.

Sloane shrugged off the comment, fully aware none of his family had taken to his first really serious relationship. "When she got the results back, the doctor suggested I have the tests." He turned then.

"I thought she was crazy, but I believed I loved her, and it seemed a simple enough way to set her mind at rest."

"You got a second opinion?" Stryker inserted roughly.

Sloane's lips twisted into a grim parody of a smile. "And a third. Same answer. No possibility of children. I just don't have what it takes."

Slater exploded out of his chair then. "Damn it to hell! Don't say that. You're better father material than either one of us. Hell, we should know. We grew up with you and all your damn lame ducks and needy people. Who started Beginning Now and bullied all of us into getting involved? Who crams knowledge into the kids? *I* sure as hell don't."

"And I wouldn't even attempt it," Stryker added, less hostilely but no less truthfully.

Slater rammed a hand through his hair and took an irritable turn around the room. "Does Eve know?"

"Yes." Sloane sat down again. Slater, when he got going, used up enough energy for all of them. He hadn't thought he could find anything amusing in this moment, but he discovered he was wrong as Slater picked up a newspaper, the only handy missile within range, and threw it at the wall. Papers fluttered around the room. He kicked at one before swinging back to them. "Why did you wait until now to tell us?" A new thought struck, tightening his features into an expression of pain. "Damn you. I don't even want to think what having our two wives around right now has cost you."

Stryker followed the train of thought. "I'll second that. Damn, Sloane, why didn't you say something?"

"For this very reason. You would have felt you had to hide the fact that Joy and Tempest were pregnant. You would have been uncomfortable. So would they. I didn't want pity and I refuse to be shut out of this kind of sharing. We've all been too close for that."

"Does Mike know?"

Sloane glanced at Slater. "No, and I will never tell him and I want your promises that you won't, either."

"You can't do that."

"Yes, I can."

Stryker hadn't taken his eyes from Sloane's face. "He's right, Slater. Mike won't handle this well at all. You know he'd figure a way to make it his fault somehow. He's been mother and father to us for too long not to rip his heart out with guilt."

Slater frowned, thinking. "Maybe," he conceded finally. "But you know he's going to drive Sloane nuts about grandkids. How are we going to get around that?"

Stryker thrust his fingers through his hair, the McGuire sign of frustration uncannily duplicated time after time. "I don't know."

"You're the problem solver," Slater reminded him.

"Well, I'm fresh out of ideas," he said, his frustration spilling out in his reply. He, too, got to his feet.

Sloane watched the pair, feeling a large measure of his pain die. Eve had been right. He should have told his brothers long ago. "Fortunately, we don't have to think of a solution right now," he pointed out. Both men swung around to glare at him as though he were speaking out of turn.

"You will be married in less than a week. Both of us speak from experience. Mike is going to be counting days. And there is no way you'll be able to get mad at him. That hopeful look in his eyes has a way of killing that idea before it can get strong enough to do you any good."

"I'll think of something. Eve's talking of adopting."

"Mike won't mind that, but he won't buy it as a substitute for your own blood."

"Too bad we can't get him married so he can breed a new set of McGuires," Slater muttered.

Sloane found a laugh. "If that's your idea of a solution, forget it. Mike assured me less than a month ago he had no intentions of ever getting married again. He'd probably have apoplexy if you suggested the idea."

Slater contemplated the picture, then grinned. "It would be worth it just to see his face."

"You shouldn't have said anything to him," Stryker pointed out to Sloane. "You know he can't resist pulling the tail of the lion." Stryker glanced at his brother. "Just remember, neither Sloane nor I will save your bacon this time. You rattle his cage at your own risk."

Slater's grin widened. "Think I can't do the deed without getting my fingers rapped?"

Sloane listened to the mock fight, knowing his brothers were giving him the only gift they could in this moment, an easy out to a difficult conversation. They had aligned themselves squarely on his side.

Slater would plot and scheme. Stryker would sift through any number of solutions. They would leave no stone unturned to help him. He loved them for the effort that would change nothing in the end. They knew as he did, this was one time the McGuires as one could not prevail. But that wouldn't stop them from trying.

"Are you sure you two don't want to come in?" Eve asked, striving to hide her weariness.

Joy shook her head as she pulled the last parcel from the back of the Blazer. "No. Tempest and I are going back to Sloane's house and take a nap so we'll have the energy for tonight's cookout. Now that we've finally found the dress . . ."

"And everything else," Eve added, interrupting.

"We can afford to be lazy."

"You don't have to come with me tomorrow to pick it up."

"Tempest has her heart set on taking you out for a big lunch before your family arrives."

Both women looked through the back window to where Tempest dozed in the front seat. For once her fire was dimmed by the effort she had put into helping Eve get ready.

"I don't know how to thank either of you for what you've done."

Joy frowned. "Don't be an ass. We love Sloane. We would have been prepared to take to anyone who made him happy. But we never needed that excuse. We like you for yourself. We did this because we wanted to."

Eve risked touching this woman who rarely

touched anyone else. "The McGuires were really lucky in their choices of wives."

Joy looked down at Eve's hand on her arm, then back to the eyes that seemed to have seen more of the darkness of life's shadows than most and yet still managed to light with innocence, hope, and trust. Joy could have envied her that, but she found instead that, like Sloane and the rest of her adopted family, she wanted to protect the very things that made Eve so strong. "Sloane picked a winner himself," she murmured, leaning forward to kiss Eve's cheek, a gesture she had given to no one else in her life. The flash of pleasure and knowledge in Eve's eyes was almost embarrassing. Joy stepped back, breaking the physical tie. "Now, I'd better get Tempest home before Stryker comes looking for us and finds her sleeping in the truck. I'm not sure even Slater could protect me if Stryker thought I let her get too tired."

"I can't believe she didn't tell us she was feeling sick."

Joy shrugged, accustomed to Tempest's steel backbone and bone-deep determination. "You can't change her. The best you can do is try to outthink her, and that rarely works." She walked around to get into the truck. She cast one comprehensive look over Tempest's relaxed body. "Her color's back and she hasn't got one thing she has to do until tonight and even that won't be much of a drain with Stryker and Sloane doing the cooking while we women get to criticize the efforts."

"What's Slater going to be doing?"

"He's clean up." She grinned. "Neither one of

us can cook a lick. If we didn't have a good house-
keeper we'd starve.''

"Sounds like you found a good compromise."

Joy started the truck. "That's the only way marriage works in reality."

Eve stepped back and waved Joy off. For the first
time in days she had some time to herself to think.
Compromise. There were solutions to Sloane's situation just as there were to her own. He had narrowed
the range with his need of a child of his own blood.
That was the stumbling block. She entered the house,
thinking of the phrase. It was a litany that haunted
her. She curled onto the couch, leaving the few pack-
ages she had brought in huddled at the door. Sloane
had offered one alternative that had surprised her.
He had been so vehement when she had first suggested it. It was a measure of his need to protect
her that he would consider the artificial insemination.
From all she had read, most men tended to shy from
that course as being an open admission to a lack
within themselves. Adoption was better, for it allowed outsiders the doubt of just who the barren
party was, or even if there were one. She grimaced
at the word *barren*. Such an emptiness, an arid
wasteland that had to hurt just by being. She couldn't
allow Sloane's suffering. Maybe she had been wrong
to refuse his solution. But knowing his father, his
brothers, and their wives, she understood their commitment to family. If only . . .

Suddenly, she sat up straight, her face pale as an
idea so farfetched slammed into her mind. Of
Sloane's own blood. His brothers, clone of him in

almost every way genetically. Triplets. Close in mind and body. Carbon copies in looks.

"I can't be thinking this," she whispered to the empty room. But which one. Slater or Stryker as the donor? Always the knowledge of parenting would live between them all. She couldn't bear it if one day the gift of a child for Sloane could destroy this family she was coming to love more with each passing day. And what of Joy and Tempest? They would have to be told. What would they feel if one of their husbands did this for his brother? How would they feel about her?

"I can't ask one of them for this," she murmured, realizing the enormity of the problems both present and future. "But how can I not ask it?" She rose and walked to the window. Sloane could have his child and she would have the joy of bearing it, but she wasn't sure either of them would be able to live with knowing what they had asked of either Slater or Stryker.

"What are we going to do?" Slater demanded when he and Stryker were finally alone.

Stryker dropped into a chair, looking defeated in a way he rarely did. "I don't know. I don't see a way out."

"You know he wants children. You can see it in his face. Damn, our timing couldn't have been worse. Why did we think dropping in like this to share the latest news of an impending addition was a good idea?"

"Joy needs that sense of family. And Tempest was getting antsy. Both of us were thinking of our women. Just as Sloane is. He didn't say anything, but we both know how his mind works. It's a good bet a lot of his pain is because he can't give Eve children. She's clearly Sloane's counterpart in that regard. Plus she's deaf. That's one loss. Sloane is probably seeing his sterility as the second. He won't like that one bit."

"It will eat at him," Slater stated bluntly. He raked his fingers through his hair. "Damn, what a mess!"

"I wonder if he's thought of artificial insemination?"

Slater shifted uncomfortably. "It's an answer."

"Eve might not go for it."

"She loves him. He said she considered adoption an option."

"Not the same thing and we both know it. The bottom line is the child wouldn't be Sloane's."

"It would be half hers. An adopted child wouldn't even be that."

"Sounds good on paper, but think about it."

"None of us is likely to do anything but think about it," Slater muttered. "I'm just glad Mike's out of our hair for a while escorting Gay and visiting with Eve's family."

"I'll second that," Stryker agreed. "The way all of us feel right now I wouldn't give us a snowball's chance in Hades of keeping this under wraps."

"Under wraps or not, we're going to have to come up with something to keep Mike off Sloane's back. He's not thinking on all cylinders if he believes Mike will be satisfied with some pap as an excuse for no children. I don't see how Sloane figures to keep this from our nosy parent.''

"I don't either." Stryker glanced at his watch. "But right now, you and I have a larger problem. Unless I'm losing my touch, I think I just heard Joy pull into the drive."

Slater glanced out the window. "It's her, and from the looks of it, your wife is sacked out in the front seat."

Stryker joined him, glaring at the scene. "I told her not to wear herself out." He headed for the door, muttering curses.

Slater followed more slowly, putting off until the last second telling Joy about Sloane. His wife was capable of feeling at long last. She would hurt for his brother and he hated the thought. But he loved them both too much to deny either with lies and evasions.

"I really don't feel like going out this morning," Eve murmured as she faced Joy in the hall. Tempest was waiting in the truck for them to set out on their last trip into town before the wedding. She put her heart into trying not to sound or look as healthy as she felt. Her plan had been born in the wee hours of the morning, when Sloane had slept beside her. They had shared so much in the night, the telling his brothers, the relief he felt that they knew, the support they had given so freely. He had seemed more at peace about his sterility than Eve had ever seen him. Sloane had told her that Slater and Stryker had told their wives, but nothing in Joy's attitude indicated that she knew.

Joy frowned, knowing an evasion when she heard one but unwilling to call Eve on it. She had no doubt Sloane had told her that Slater and Stryker would share Sloane's situation with their wives. Perhaps Eve was feeling awkward with the whole. Certainly she and Tempest were treading carefully.

"What about the fitting?"

"I was hoping you wouldn't mind calling and changing the appointment for me."

"Are you sure?"

Eve made herself smile weakly. "Yes. I'll nap for a little while, then I'll meet you two for lunch as we planned. Besides, you don't really need me to find a maternity dress for Tempest."

Hearing the last of the excuse, Joy thought she understood the reason for the flimsy excuse to stay home. Neither she nor Tempest had remembered the final reason that this trip to town was so important when they had driven over to pick up Eve. "All right. Let me tell Tempest the change in plans and I'll make your call. Then we'll be on our way."

Eve's smile was more relieved than she knew, reinforcing Joy's belief. "I'll be fine by lunch," she promised.

Less than ten minutes later, Eve watched the Blazer ease down the street, heading for town. She waited an extra ten to make certain, then left the house. She wanted to reach Sloane's house before Stryker and Slater took off on their own pursuits for the day. With Sloane at the University for the morning, she would never have a better time to broach her plan. She was trembling with nerves by the time she walked the three blocks that separated the two houses. Her knock was answered on the first try.

"Eve?" Slater stared at Eve's pale face, then looked beyond her to the empty drive. He caught her hands, chafing at the cold fingers. "What is it? Did you have an accident? Where are Joy and Tempest?"

"They went into town without me," she said, holding on to his warmth. "I needed to talk to you and Stryker alone. Is he still here?" Her eyes held his, pleading without her realizing it.

Slater's frown deepened as he drew her inside the house and shut the door. "In the kitchen wrapped around a cup of coffee." He urged her down the hall.

Stryker looked no less startled than Slater when Eve entered the kitchen ahead of Slater.

Because Eve had her back to him, Slater took advantage of her deafness to warn his brother. "She sent the women into town so she could see us alone. Look at her. Something's happened."

Stryker accepted the words without a change of expression. He rose and pulled out a chair for Eve. "A cup of tea."

She laughed shakily. "A good stiff whiskey sounds a lot better. I'm going to need it before this morning is over."

The men exchanged disturbed looks behind her back.

"I'll make the tea," Slater muttered. "You're more a listener than I ever was."

Stryker sat and took Eve's cold hand in his. "Whatever it is, we'll do our best to help."

Eve searched his eyes. There wasn't much to

choose between the men in looks unless one studied their eyes. The heart of each McGuire triplet lay in the dark depths for those discerning enough to search for the soul of the man. She was banking on that soul she had glimpsed in each of them now. She gathered her courage and prayed she wasn't making the greatest mistake of her life. Her future with Sloane could be shattered in the next few minutes or she could paint a golden path to Sloane's impossible dream. She had never been more conscious of the all-or-nothing choice she had made.

"I want to give Sloane what he wants more than almost anything in the world. And I need your help to do it."

"A child."

"More than that. A child of his blood."

Stryker knew that if he needed a picture of raw courage he was looking at it now. This woman loved his brother enough to risk more than he knew to give Sloane what fate had denied him. "How?"

"Artificial insemination. You and Slater as donors."

Slater sat down beside her and pushed a cup near her right hand. "We thought of that. Either one of us will do it, but I don't think Sloane will go for it."

"Not *either*." She took a shallow breath, praying she had chosen rightly. "Both of you."

"What?" Slater demanded. He was too shocked to remember to wait until she looked at him to speak.

Stryker shook his head, holding on to his own emotions long enough to listen to her reasoning. "Why both?"

"It's the baby," Eve explained in a rush, now that she had gotten over the first hurdle. "If only one of you is the donor, all of us will know the donor is the father. Your wife, whichever one, me, Sloane, either of you. We would have the best of intentions, but that knowledge would always be there. But if there was a mix of . . ." She hesitated over the word, then forced it out. ". . . sperm, there would be no way to tell without specialized tests. This way we could all look at it as donating a bit of essence to make a child. Not the child itself. It would be the McGuire blood and seed as Sloane calls it. Wouldn't that make it easier on all of us?" Her grip tightened on his, begging him to see what it had taken her hours to discover. "Would it be so very different this way from both of you donating bone marrow or something like that to the other? You wouldn't have to think of it as giving me a child. It would be giving Sloane the strength of your blood. The baby could be his because it couldn't be claimed by either of you for certain."

Stryker looked at his brother, thinking of the sacrifice in pride Eve was making. He saw the same knowledge living in Slater's dark eyes.

Eve hurried on. She had tried to cover every angle to protect all of them. She could not take her happiness, knew Sloane would not accept his at his family's expense. "I would even sign a paper, a legal document that said that if something happened to our marriage, I would give up all rights to the child. It is McGuire blood to be raised by the McGuires. You won't have to worry about Sloane ever losing his child by my hand," she vowed, giving her last ounce of strength to the pledge. Tears stood in her eyes, but she didn't notice. "That way, what you do would be strictly for him."

Slater touched her shoulder, feeling the tension that had her delicate body strung tight enough to break. This time he waited until she looked at him to speak. "Have you thought of what Sloane will say to this?" The man he believed his brother to be would not accept their help for the very reasons that Eve had already pointed out.

"I'm afraid of what he will say," she admitted. "He hurt so much for himself in the beginning, but now mostly because of me. I have to help him." She gripped his hand. "Don't you understand? If I were not deaf it would be easier. He feels he is taking something from me that he has no right to steal. I have lost enough." The last sentence spilled out with the bitterness that Sloane had taught her could exist in her world.

Neither man looked ready to agree. Her hope sank into a sea of broken dreams. Only the memory of how often she had looked defeat in the face and triumphed in the end kept her from running out of the room. She had to believe in these two so like the man she loved. She turned back to Stryker. "I don't expect your answers now. But will you at least think about it?"

"We love him, too."

A tiny bit of the tension that had locked her muscles to the point of pain drained away. "Knowing that was the only thing that gave me courage enough to ask this of you both."

"If we do decide that we can do this, let us tell him."

She shook her head, rejecting the risk he would run for her. "No. My choice. My idea. My right to face him with what I have asked of you."

Slater shook his head as he caught Eve's shoulder, bringing her around to face him. "No. Stryker's right. Let us tell him."

"I won't let something I did come between you."

"And we won't let you put yourself on the chopping block."

She smiled at the vehemence she could see rather than hear. "You can't stop me."

"She's got you there," Stryker pointed out.

Slater glared at her, admiring her courage even if it was damn inconvenient. "He needs you."

"He needs the hope of this baby as well."

"Without you he won't have even that. I can't think of another woman who would do this for him. And I don't mean carrying another man's seed to give her husband a child."

Eve touched his hand. "If she loved enough she would do even more. Take a bullet, perhaps. Turn away from the only joy in her life because it was a ride with death at her shoulder," she replied, reminding both men of their own wives. "Women have spent their history going to the wall for their men. It is one of our greatest strengths."

Neither man could deny her claim. They lived with and loved their own proof.

"We'll compromise. We'll think about it."

Feeling exhausted but at peace as well, Eve rose. Stryker pushed to his feet. "I'll drive you home."

Slater held her still for a moment. "Our wives will have to know."

Eve looked surprised. "Of course. It is their right and their decision as well as yours."

Slater released her, shaking his head. She was so determined, so strong, when she looked as if a good breeze would send her to Canada. He wondered if Sloane even realized Eve's power. No wonder Joy and Tempest had taken to her. They had recognized a kindred soul.

THIRTEEN

Sloane studied his brothers as they faced him across the width of the desk. The women were upstairs sleeping. Tomorrow was the rehearsal dinner and Eve's family was arriving in the morning. The last thing Sloane wanted to be doing was eating up his precious moments of solitude with Eve. "What was so important that the two of you needed me to stay here so late? Eve's waiting for me."

"We know," Slater agreed. "That's what we wanted to talk to you about. Stryker and I have something that we want to give you for a wedding present."

Sloane's brows rose at the tone that seemed more tense than glad. "At this hour?"

Stryker took over the explanations. Slater still wasn't comfortable going against Eve's wishes. "We've been thinking about your problem."

Sloane stiffened, his gaze focused on his brother's face.

"We have a solution. It's a bit unorthodox, but we think it will serve."

"I don't want to get into this," Sloane stated flatly.

"Well, you damn well better," Slater inserted bluntly.

Stryker gestured Slater to silence. "Have you thought of artificial insemination?"

"Eve won't go for it. She says I'd be doing it only for her."

Stryker inclined his head at the confirmation of what Eve had told them. "You wouldn't be if the child carried our blood."

Sloane knew Stryker wasn't teasing him. It wasn't in the man's nature to be cruel. "Meaning?"

"Slater and I will be the donors."

Sloane inhaled deeply at the solution he hadn't even considered. He thought of what the gift would mean to him, to Eve, to their family. Even as the hope glittered with fool's-gold promise, he knew he would not accept their offer. "One of you would do that?"

"Hell, we'd do a lot more," Slater assured him gruffly.

His refusal had to be gentle. Their attempt to solve the impossible deserved that and more. "But my child would really be yours, and you'd know it."

"Not if we donated a mixture of sperm. Without some very specialized tests there would be no way any of us could know for certain."

Sloane stared at him as though he had just landed from outer space. Every coherent thought slipped away.

"Don't just sit there," Slater commanded irritably. "Say something."

"That's got to be the craziest reasoning I've ever heard. I can't believe either one of you came up with this idea."

Slater shifted in his chair. Stryker didn't blink. Sloane caught both reactions. He knew them too well. Suddenly, he knew. Before he could think, his reaction surged past his control. Anger blazed in his eyes, his words. "It wasn't your idea at all." Eve had said it wouldn't matter. "She had no right to drag you two into this. Why did you let her?"

"It's a good plan. The wives agreed completely."

Sloane surged to his feet, needing to expend his energy on something more civilized than slamming his fist through a wall. "You talked to them?"

Slater stood, facing Sloane's anger. "We damn well aren't doing it without their agreement. You wouldn't without talking to Eve and you know it."

Sloane jammed his balled-up fists on the desk. "I wouldn't have talked to Eve without first seeing how you felt about it. We aren't talking about getting a puppy here."

Stryker got to his feet, no less angry than the other two but considerably more controlled. "If you think it was easy on any of us, think again. It's a touchy subject for anyone. We can't understand completely what you're feeling, but give us credit for trying. As for us telling you instead of Eve, that was our idea. Both Slater and I agreed that you would need to blow off steam and she doesn't deserve to bear the brunt of the McGuire temper."

"What did you think I was going to do? Beat her for coming up with a harebrained plan?"

"If you'd stop thinking with your emotions and look at it logically you'd see it isn't harebrained at all. What's the difference between us donating some sperm for you and doing something like a bone marrow transplant if you had an illness that needed that kind of treatment?"

Sloane raked his fingers through his hair, feeling driven into a corner. "I don't know what the difference is, but there is one."

"Only because of the sensitive nature of the problem," Stryker said flatly, refusing to back down.

"That still doesn't make it right." Sloane stalked to the door.

"Where are you going?" Slater demanded, taking a step toward him as though to follow.

Sloane's look mocked his big-brother tactics. "Where do you think? To talk to my meddling fiancée."

Stryker caught his arm. "At least wait until you calm down."

"That might be years from now." Sloane jerked out of his hold. "But don't worry, I won't even yell." He strode through the door and out of the house.

"He won't need to yell," Slater muttered. "He does better with a soft tone than anyone I know."

Stryker inclined his head, his expression deeply disturbed. "I wish we had one of those boxes on the phone so we could call Eve and warn her."

"We didn't do a very good job of telling him."

Stryker looked at him. "Do you really think there

is a way to touch something like this without stirring up a tidal wave? I wouldn't have handled it any better, and neither would you.''

Slater shrugged uncomfortably. ''Maybe Eve can calm him down. Now that I've thought about it, I think it's the only way for Sloane. His woman is one gutsy lady.''

''She's going to need every bit of it tonight.''

The lights indicating someone was at the door blinked insistently. Eve frowned. Sloane had a key, and he was the only one she was expecting. Drawing her robe close around her, she went to the door and peered through the peephole. The sight of Sloane's face deepened her frown. As she let him in, she said, ''Why didn't you use your key?''

Sloane stalked into the living room before he turned around to face her. The walk between their two houses had done nothing to cool his temper and he wanted to be cool. He wanted to hear her side. ''I just had an interesting talk with Stryker and Slater.''

Eve stared at him, feeling the waves of anger pouring off him in an almost tangible force. Her stomach tightened as she searched his eyes. They had told him. There was no other explanation.

''No denials?''

''There isn't any point.'' She crossed her arms over her breasts, feeling on trial but determined not to break.

''You had no right.''

''In two days I will bear your name. Your troubles become mine as mine become yours. Are you telling me you wouldn't go to any lengths to help me if I needed something? I won't believe you."

"You sound like them. This isn't something that simple."

"Emotionally, I agree. There are all kinds of feelings tied up here. But they want to do it. It's a solution, and Joy and Tempest have agreed. The child will carry your blood." Her arms dropping out of their defensive position, she closed the distance so that she could touch him. "You worried about what I would lose. I wanted to give you a way to have what you wanted."

"And give yourself a way to have a baby by a McGuire." He didn't want to believe this of her, but the past had taught him hard lessons. Trust needed time to mature. They simply had not had that time.

She drew back, her hand hovering just above his arm, his warmth. Cold whispered around her. "You can't believe that was my motive," she breathed in a voice that almost wasn't there.

"Can't I? I offered you artificial insemination. You refused."

"I told you why. Because your reasons were only for me. It isn't enough."

"Maybe. Maybe not. I won't know now, will I?"

"What do you mean?"

Sloane studied her, the eyes that were filled with tears that even now she wouldn't shed. He might have respected her more if she cried. He didn't know. He only knew that as he watched his brothers offer him a lifeline, learning that cord was woven by Eve to reach into a future he had thought lost, he had known rage such as never before.

"I mean, wife to be, I'll take your gift. I want a child as much if not more than you do. But don't think I will ever forget that it was your idea."

Eve's hand dropped. She couldn't have touched him now if her life depended on the gesture. She hadn't known she could feel such pain, such betrayal. It didn't matter to him that she had been willing to sign the child away if they parted. He hadn't seen the gesture as her promise that it was he she wanted, not the promise of his seed in her womb. She backed away, each step carefully controlled, precise.

"For as long as I am here, this is my home. I want you to leave." She spaced each word, enunciating it as though her existence depended on its formation.

Sloane frowned at her, ripped from his temper by something terrible in her face. He took a step toward her. She answered with three quick ones back. Fear fused with the anger. "We're getting married in two days," he reminded her.

She shook her head. "No."

Sloane wanted to lash out. He stifled the urge, fighting for control as he never had. "And I say we are."

"You can't force me down the aisle."

"No, but I can tell your family and mine why you're backing out," he replied roughly.

"You won't do that."

He did steal the yards between them then, catching her shoulders to keep her from retreating still more. "Try me. I mean to have you and our child that you have gone to so much trouble to make possible." He bent his head until his lips captured hers. Words wouldn't do the job. But neither of them could deny the passion. His kiss was hot, a rage of emotions that needed an outlet and an answering blaze of feeling. He got both. Her hands dug into his hair, binding him as tightly as his hands held her. When he lifted his head they were both breathing hard.

"This doesn't change a thing," she gasped. "I still won't have you."

His smile was steel-edged and held no forgiveness for either of them. "We'll see." He released her and headed for the door. "Come, lock me out."

Eve followed more slowly. He didn't even pause as he walked into the night.

"Eve, won't you tell me what's wrong?" Gay asked, studying her sister's wan face. "When I left here, you were all but glowing. Now you look like death walking."

"I have a headache."

"You don't get them."

Eve put down her coffee cup and started to get up. Gay's hand on her arm stopped her.

"Don't shut me out. I know I hurt your feelings but please don't shut me out."

It took a moment for Eve even to remember what Gay was talking about. "I have forgotten," she said honestly.

"Then talk to me. Maybe I can help."

Eve smiled sadly. "There has been too much helping already." When Gay looked ready to argue, she added, "There really isn't anything you can do anyway."

Gay searched her expression. "You're sure?"

"Very." She made herself sit down again. If she didn't get a hold on herself her whole family would be demanding to know what was going on. She couldn't think how to get out of the mess she had made. She couldn't face walking down the aisle, but equally she couldn't risk Sloane exposing his problem in front of everyone as he threatened. She shouldn't have cared. But all she could think of was the bleak despair she had seen so often in his eyes. She loved him. His misjudgment didn't change that. And how she was going to live with him or without him she didn't know.

"The parents were really thrilled about the wedding in spite of the speed. Mom is over the moon," Gay said, hoping to distract Eve. "If they hadn't had so much to do, both of them would have been here to help the day I told them."

Eve forced herself to concentrate. "Joy and Tempest have stepped into the breach, believe me."

Gay grinned. "I like them both. And their husbands."

If she didn't think of Sloane, she wouldn't hurt so much. "I think you just plain like the McGuires, by marriage or blood."

Gay laughed, something she had done rarely until becoming entangled with the McGuire clan. "Mom said the same thing."

Eve saw the new happiness in her sister's face. At least Gay had gotten something good out of their time in North Carolina. "You deserve a little of the pleasure in life."

"Well, I sure am tired of the gray. I don't know how you put up with me all this time."

"When you love someone you can accept a lot."

Those words echoed in Eve's mind as she went through the motions of the day, the excitement of her family meeting the McGuires en masse. The luncheon filled with talk and laughter. The scramble for bathroom space as everyone got ready for the rehearsal and the dinner following. Both Stryker and Slater had come to her, apologizing for their interference and expressing their relief that they had done no lasting damage since Sloane had agreed to the insemination and the wedding was still on. She had managed to get through the interview and the searching looks both men had turned on her. But it had cost her dearly for every evasion, every white lie. So the pretense continued, and in all the chaos, no one seemed to notice that the prospective bride and groom were putting on a show. Sloane's smile was as fixed as her own. His arm held her without the tenderness that she had come to expect. His kiss was hot with controlled anger and hurt. She wanted to stroke away the pain and the betrayal that blazed out of his eyes, but she couldn't forget what he thought of her. The knowledge was a slow acid in her heart, eating away to her soul.

"I can't do it," she whispered as she waited for the rehearsal to begin. She stood in the darkness of the alcove of the church surrounded by the members of her bridal party—Joy, Tempest, and Gay. Eve glanced out over the church. The Lucks were there, Pippa and her husband Josh. Eve's family had business dealings with Josh, and Eve had met him a few times in the beginning of that association, in a time before Pippa. It had been a surprise to learn that the

Pippa who the McGuires cared so much for was
Josh's wife. Her gaze traveled over the rest of the
congregation. The Richlands were also present,
Christiana and her husband and their two children.
Her family. The McGuires. The place was packed.
Eve put a hand to her stomach. She just couldn't go
through with it no matter what Sloane threatened.
She stared at his rigid back for one second, then
turned to Gay.

"I'm not feeling well."

Gay caught her hand, rubbing it, frowning at the
coldness of her touch. "You look like milk." She
put an arm around Eve's shoulders and urged her
toward the small dressing area down the hall. "I'll
tell Sloane."

"No, I don't want him to know," Eve blurted.

Gay froze, exchanging a look with Joy. "You'd
better get him."

After one sharp look, Joy nodded and left quickly.

Eve shook off Gay's hand. "You shouldn't have
done that."

Before Gay could reply, Sloane was there.
"Would you leave us alone?"

After a searching look at Eve's white face and
Sloane's rigid one, Gay murmured an agreement and
went out, closing the door behind her.

Sloane leaned against the panel and studied Eve.
She did look ill. He hadn't meant to do that to her
no matter what she had done to him. Irritated with
the guilt he felt, he tried to remember why he was
angry, what she had attempted. "Cold feet?"

"I won't do it." She linked her fingers tightly

together as she faced him. "I won't make promises that have no meaning."

"They have meaning."

"Not for you." She watched his eyes, praying that he would finally see why she had approached his brothers with her plan. When she found no softness in his look, no forgiveness in his expression, her chin lifted, her own anger beating back the misery of guilt and anxiety. She had been condemned, but she would not die with a whimper. "How can you think that I would put either of us through this just for myself? I thought you understood me better than that." Tears filled her eyes, but she held them back. She would cry buckets and rivers later but not now. "Do you have any idea how hard it was for me to talk to Slater and Stryker? Or to promise to sign a legal document giving you our baby unconditionally if something happened between us? I love that child already, and it's only a hope in my heart."

Sloane stilled, every muscle going rigid as her words sank in. "What legal document?" he demanded urgently, harshly.

Eve hardly heard him. "Stryker and Slater said you wouldn't want such a thing. Even when I assured them my lawyer would swallow his tongue before he betrayed a confidence, they still thought it was unnecessary. But I didn't want you to think I was like those other women. I wanted you to know the baby was my gift to our future. Not mine. Not yours. But ours." The tears flowed faster now, blinding her and sealing her in silence that couldn't be broken by words. "I failed," she whispered, her voice more a sob than words. She had thought herself strong enough not to break. She discovered that Sloane was the one thing on the face of the earth to bring her to her knees. "I loved you more than anyone and I hurt you so much."

Sloane jerked away from the door, her suffering getting past his own. Her words snatched him back from the jaws of his dark past. Light was around her, just as it had always been. He had been blind for a while, blinded by his pain just as she was blinded by her tears now. His prison had been as complete as her own. He pulled her into his arms, ignoring her resistance. He tucked her head against his heart and let the pain flow out of both of them in the silver streams of her grief. He held her, thanking every god he believed in that this woman had found him. Her gift of a child wasn't nearly as important as the strength of her love. He would cherish both all the days of his life and hers.

He raised her head, his fingers under her chin. His lips dried the tears from her face so that she could see. "I love you. No one told me about the paper. And I shouldn't have needed that anyway. I should have trusted you. That will always be my regret. And nothing I can say will ever take back what I said to you last night, what I threatened. Forgive me, Eve. So I can begin to live with myself." He didn't wait for the words he demanded. His anger had been a dam shattered by her tears. He gave because he had no choice if he was to keep her, to write all their tomorrows in her language, the one she had taught him to speak. He traced the track of one tear down her cheek. "My brothers were right. I don't need a written guarantee because nothing will happen. We are our future. And our child, made of your body, born of your love and mine, will be our tomorrow.'' He kissed her tenderly, begging without sound as only a man with his strength could do. ''Say you will forgive me for what I almost did to us.''

She searched his eyes, reading the truth. He hadn't known. She remembered those who had come before her and the wounds they had inflicted. That memory and the scars he carried made forgiveness possible. ''I forgive you if you will forgive yourself. Promise me no more shadows.''

He cupped her face in his palms. ''You know me too well.''

''Your promise,'' she whispered.

''You have it. Anything you ask of me, I'll move heaven and hell to give you.''

''I'll be spoiled.''

His smile touched her almost as tenderly as his lips had. ''Not on your worst day, Saint Eve.''

She tipped back her head, her eyes dancing with a challenge and the love that had been shrouded in darkness and pain for a time. She was free. He had broken the last chain that would have imprisoned her in darkness too deep to light. ''You like to live dangerously.''

''It's a family trait which our offspring will probably inherit.'' He kissed the smile on her lips, tasting it, sharing his own with her. When he raised his head, he tucked her arm in the crook of his. ''Come on, let's get this marriage on the road so we can make our baby.''

''I do like your style, Sloane McGuire.''

He opened the door to find a sea of worried faces. He looked down at her, smiling. "I think they figured you were going to leave me at the altar."

"Not a chance," Eve denied, grinning at the assemblage. "I caught you and I'm keeping you, come hell or high water."

EPILOGUE

The corridor in front of the nursery was crowded with people, each one jostling for a position to view the occupant of the pink-decked crib in center front. The squalling little red-faced baby girl didn't care who was looking. She was stuck in a bright world of alien sounds and cold like none she had experienced and she was not happy with the process that involved a lot of pushing and pulling on her small body. Her voice rose in a wail.

Her audience grinned as though she had done something truly extraordinary. If she had been able to talk she would have informed them that she had only just started getting even with the world. Colic sounded like a good way to make those around her aware of her displeasure. Teething was even better. And the fun of burping down one of those talking giants' backs ranked high on the list of retaliations. She couldn't wait. But first she had to get something to eat. Her fist waved angrily in the air as she tried to reach her mouth.

"That kid has a pair of lungs on her," Mike informed the audience at large. "Sloane did well."

Slater slapped his father on the back. "You said that about Stryker when Jennifer was born."

Stryker duplicated the gesture. "And when Amanda was born."

Mike shook his head. "I can't understand it. I had three boys and you three had girls and you only got one each."

Sloane joined the admiring pack. "That's because we're not the man our father is," he said with a grin that held not one shadow of darkness.

"Well, Daddy, how is Mother?" Slater demanded.

"Doing great, although she is complaining because they won't let her come out here where all the action is."

"Eve better enjoy her rest while she can," Joy said with a laugh. "Our niece looks like she's going to run you both ragged. Thank goodness Amanda doesn't take after her."

Tempest tucked her arm in Stryker's. "You noticed that, too? Jennifer was really quiet in the nursery. It must be Sloane's temper."

Sloane laughed. He would never be able to repay the four in front of him for what they had given him and Eve. And it had been a real gift. Not by look, tone, or word had any of them ever referred to the day that Eve had been impregnated with the McGuire mix.

"You better get back to Eve before she decides to come down here in spite of orders," Stryker said.

"She would, too," Sloane agreed with a chuckle.

"She's got the devil's own determination when she wants to do something." He was still smiling when he entered Eve's room to find her glaring at the ceiling.

Although she couldn't hear him, Eve knew that he had come to her. Her ill temper cleared immediately and her lips curved up as he leaned down to kiss her. "Did you see her?"

He nodded and eased down on the bed beside her hip. "She's yelling her head off. Joy and Tempest said they could see that she got her disposition from me."

She touched his cheek, knowing how much their collective attitude meant to him. Their child was truly theirs. The gift of life had been perfect in its giving. Their baby had been conceived in a love made strong by more than just two. Temper or no, she would be a very special child, cherished by her and Sloane in ways that ordinary parents would never know.

"I love you."

He touched her cheek, looking into those eyes that saw more clearly, more fearlessly, than most. "I can't tell you how much I love you. You have given me tomorrow and all the days after that."

"What shall we name her? We never decided."

He traced her lips. "Faith. Your faith in me, in us, in my brothers, in our future brought her to us."

"You give me too much credit." She raised up to take his mouth. She needed him as she needed no other. He alone saw her as a whole woman, strong enough to take her place at his side, a full partner in all that they worked for, dreamed for, and planned.

Sloane gathered her in his arms. She would never see her strength in all its guises. He understood that about her, accepted it and held it dear. She was his life and the light that made living more than just survival. She colored his days, his thoughts. Even that she didn't fully understand. But it didn't matter. Nothing mattered more than the joy of holding her in his arms, knowing she belonged only to him for all time.

SHARE THE FUN . . .
SHARE YOUR NEW-FOUND TREASURE!!

You don't want to let your new books out of your sight? That's okay. Your friends can get their own. Order below.

No. 35 DIAMOND ON ICE by Lacey Dancer
Diana could melt even the coldest of hearts. Jason hasn't a chance.

No. 59 13 DAYS OF LUCK by Lacey Dancer
Author Pippa Weldon finds her real-life hero in Joshua Luck.

No. 98 BABY MAKES FIVE by Lacey Dancer
Cait could say 'no' to his business offer but not to Robert, the man.

No. 127 FOREVER JOY by Lacey Dancer
Joy was a riddle and Slater was determined to unravel her mystery.

No. 133 LIGHTNING STRIKES TWICE by Lacey Dancer
Stryker has spent his life rescuing Tempest. Can he finally save her?

No. 163 HIS WOMAN'S GIFT by Lacey Dancer
Eve's love of life touched Sloane and made him think, wish and remember.

No. 36 DADDY'S GIRL by Janice Kaiser
Slade wants more than Andrea is willing to give. Who wins?

No. 37 ROSES by Caitlin Randall
It's an inside job & K.C. helps Brett find more than the thief!

No. 38 HEARTS COLLIDE by Ann Patrick
Matthew finds big trouble and it's spelled P-a-u-l-a.

No. 40 CATCH A RISING STAR by Laura Phillips
Justin is seeking fame; Beth helps him find something more important.

No. 41 SPIDER'S WEB by Allie Jordan
Silvia's quiet life explodes when Fletcher shows up on her doorstep.

No. 43 DUET by Patricia Collinge
Adam & Marina fit together like two perfect parts of a puzzle!

No. 44 DEADLY COINCIDENCE by Denise Richards
J.D.'s instincts tell him he's not wrong; Laurie's heart says trust him.

No. 46 ONE ON ONE by JoAnn Barbour
Vincent's no saint but Loie's attracted to the devil in him anyway.

No. 47 STERLING'S REASONS by Joey Light
Joe is running from his conscience; Sterling helps him find peace.

No. 48 SNOW SOUNDS by Heather Williams
In the quiet of the mountain, Tanner and Melaine find each other again.

No. 51 RISKY BUSINESS by Jane Kidwell
Blair goes undercover but finds more than she bargained for with Logan.

No. 54 DAYDREAMS by Marina Palmieri
Kathy's life is far from a fairy tale. Is Jake her Prince Charming?

No. 55 A FOREVER MAN by Sally Falcon
Max is trouble and Sandi wants no part of him. She *must* resist!

No. 56 A QUESTION OF VIRTUE by Carolyn Davidson
Neither Sara nor Cal can ignore their almost magical attraction.

No. 57 BACK IN HIS ARMS by Becky Barker
Fate takes over when Tara shows up on Rand's doorstep again.

No. 60 SARA'S ANGEL by Sharon Sala
Sara *must* get to Hawk. He's the only one who can help.

No. 61 HOME FIELD ADVANTAGE by Janice Bartlett
Marian shows John there is more to life than just professional sports.

No. 62 FOR SERVICES RENDERED by Ann Patrick
Nick's life is in perfect order until he meets Claire!

Meteor Publishing Corporation
Dept. 893, P. O. Box 41820, Philadelphia, PA 19101-9828

Please send the books I've indicated below. Check or money order (U.S. Dollars only)—no cash, stamps or C.O.D.s (PA residents, add 6% sales tax). I am enclosing $2.95 plus 75¢ handling fee for *each* book ordered.

Total Amount Enclosed: $_____.

___ No. 35	___ No. 36	___ No. 44	___ No. 55
___ No. 59	___ No. 37	___ No. 46	___ No. 56
___ No. 98	___ No. 38	___ No. 47	___ No. 57
___ No. 127	___ No. 40	___ No. 48	___ No. 60
___ No. 133	___ No. 41	___ No. 51	___ No. 61
___ No. 163	___ No. 43	___ No. 54	___ No. 62

Please Print:
Name _____

Address _____ Apt. No. _____

City/State _____ Zip _____

Allow four to six weeks for delivery. Quantities limited.